ISLAND RAMPAGE

ALEX LAYBOURNE

SEVERED PRESS
Hobart Tasmania

ISLAND RAMPAGE

This book is dedicated to my wife Patty, and our five wonderful children, James, Logan, Ashleigh, Damon and Riley.

CHAPTER 1

The clouds broke, and the islands came into view. Three of them in all; a larger central location with two smaller siblings in close proximity.

Johan Krauss stared at them and smiled. His mind already spinning, ideas flying left and right. He looked down at the uninhabited oasis and saw potential. He looked at it, and he saw money.

Perhaps the most important thing in Johan's life, money made up for everything he did not have as a child. He worked hard, earning the fortune behind his name. He did not need family, nor the love of a good woman. He could buy loyalty wherever he went in the world, and to him, that was an even greater bond than anything emotional.

Women could be purchased. Memories and experiences bought, and pleasure guaranteed. The same could not be said for an emotional connection.

"Set her down on the main island, I want to take a look around," he spoke into the microphone.

"Sir, we do not have permission to land here," the pilot responded, sounding almost sheepish.

"Nonsense, Godfrey. I own these islands now, and if I want to land on them, then I will do just that." Godfrey knew better than to argue with his boss. The man always had a plan, and when all else failed, even Godfrey understood that every man had a price.

They descended, dropping closer to the small archipelago, a patch of recently discovered, unclaimed land. The race to pinpoint to exact coordinates heated up fast. In the distance, Johan could make out three different yachts, both heading in the same direction, both intent on claiming the land for themselves.

Too bad they would be trespassing on his private property the moment they stepped foot on the shore. Hell, Johan added the water surrounding the islands to his property list. He needed it if the vision in his head became reality.

"Sir, with your permission, I would like to land on that rocky outcrop among the trees, rather than on the beach. We do not know the area, and having a solid base beneath us would be imperative should we be required to exit, post haste," Godfrey spoke, as they circled the island one last time.

"Agreed. Besides, it will be a nice surprise when my competitors arrive, and find me king of the mountain." Johan smiled, rubbing his hands together as his mind played out the varying forms of rage and disappointment he expected to see on the faces of the men he had beaten.

The light cloud base did nothing to lessen the force of the weather on the island. Once beyond the protection of the chopper, the heat had free-reign to beat down on them. Combining with the moisture-rich ground, it created a sweltering, humid atmosphere, making the island feel hostile and unwelcoming. Exactly what Johan wanted.

The blades of the helicopter fell silent and the natural sounds of the island began to rise. The rustle of the trees, the hum of the ocean, and the distant, muffled sound of life.

"This way," Johan said, pointing down the rocky outcrop. He spotted the perfect location as the helicopter descended. It would serve as the foundation for the construction he had planned.

Godfrey offered no response, but swapped his pilot mentality for that of a bodyguard. A man of many talents, he had performed any job requested by Johan for almost twelve years. Without hesitation. He understood the correct order of things in life. The chain of command existed for a reason, and knowing where you stood was imperative. He tucked the 9mm pistol into the waistband of his trousers, and grabbed the machete from inside the chopper.

"Follow me, sir," he said.

When no clear path became visible, Godfrey to set to creating his own, hacking and slashing at the dense vegetation. Grasses and vines, flowers, and wild bushes blocked their path, yet they all fell victim to the blade swung in their direction.

Making slow, but steady progress, Godfrey pressed on without complaint. He swapped arms when one grew tired, and used both when the need arose.

His body was drenched with sweat when they broke free of the vegetation and entered a large clearing.

"Is this not just ideal?" Johan asked, knowing that agreement would come from his most trusted associate.

"Yes, sir, this place is full of potential," Godfrey replied, wiping his brow with a handkerchief. It proved to be as useful as trying to extinguish a house fire with a thimble of water.

"You are a good friend, Godfrey. I can always count on you. I will not forget your loyalty," Johan spoke without so much as casting a glance in the direction of the man he spoke to. His eyes held a distant gaze, staring at the spot he chose to be the cornerstone of his vision.

The laboratories would be free from the confines of the modern world. Here, they would be free to work in any way necessary to achieve results.

The same thick vegetation surrounded the rocky plateau on all sides. Above them, mountainous terrain rose into the sky, the trees thick all to the way to the flattened top.

Below them, the land sloped away, dropping down to the base level where the island stretched out with a mixture of dense forest, rocky outcrops, and a beach that rivalled anything ever captured on a postcard.

Untamed and wild, the island had the potential for anything and everything. The air buzzed with it. There was an energy to the land that could not be ignored.

To find a space, untouched by man, not yet tainted by humanity, in the modern world could be called a miracle. Johan knew this, and as he watched the approaching yachts, his heart sang. The taste of victory was sweet.

"We need to get down to the beach. I have claimed this land, and I will pay handsomely for it, if needed. Let's not let these fools get their hopes up," he spoke to Godfrey. His bodyguard stood with his back to him. His eyes set on the trees, and the mountain above them.

"Sorry, boss, did you say something?" he asked, turning.

"We need to get down to the beach," Johan repeated, a conversational practice he abhorred.

"Sure thing, anything you say." Godfrey let out a long breath. He would never admit it, but the island gave him the creeps. He could not shake the feeling that they were being watched.

His life story involved a number of unsavoury characters, and a great many unsavoury situations. In that time, Godfrey learned to trust his gut. Call it intuition, precognition, or whatever. Godfrey believed he could smell danger. It tainted the air with its presence. Not necessarily a noticeable taint, but something subtle.

Standing there, in the open, surrounded by dense forest, the stench could not be ignored. His entire body tingled with anticipation, the kind that lead directly to fear. Godfrey considered himself a brave man, a tough man, a man who would act without hesitation. Given the choice, right then and there, the only thing he would do without said hesitation, would be to leave the island and head back to the mainland. Rather, head back to the anchored yacht, which in turn, would bring them back to the mainland.

***

Charles Gallway watched the island rise up on the horizon. By his calculations, they would reach land within an hour. That gave him just enough time to brief his men, leaving the yacht in the capable hands of his first mate, a burly Irishman, known to all but Charles, as Tiny. Charles first met Eamon way back when. Two years older but close to two feet shorter, Charles took Eamon under his wing. A giant of a man, with a simple mind, it did not take much for Charles to mould Eamon to his will. Becoming inseparable as they aged, the two became a formidable force. The brains and the muscle, most people knew well enough to leave them be. Those that did not, only needed to be told once.

Below deck, the team of five sat waiting. Hired hands, brought onboard with the simple task of ensuring success. Charles had plans for the islands, and the means with which he could take control.

The five men sat in silence, the need for conversation long since passed. Having worked together for so long, the men knew their jobs, understood their role, and revelled in the thrill of the chase.

"Remember," he addressed the group, "these islands are supposed to be uninhabited. They are mine to claim. Your services are only required should we find anybody trying to claim rights ahead of us."

A disgruntled murmur rushed through the group, who, when all squashed together made the galley of the luxury yacht seem much smaller.

"Don't worry. You will be paid either way. Bloodshed or not, your presence will be rewarded. You have my word on that. I am sure you have heard the rumours, but my word is my bond, and I would never betray it." Charles looked from one man to the next, and smiled at the cold, ruthless expressions that gazed back at him.

The yacht skirted around the first of the three islands. Everybody knew that the islands were a package deal, and bragging rights revolved around claiming the large central mass.

Interest was high. Charles had already faced off against several other figures, several from Eastern Europe. They cost him three of his own man. His reasoning behind hiring the mercenaries being that he considered them expendable. His own men, not so much.

"Bring her around into the bay, Eamon," Charles instructed as they fell into the long shadows of the island's green peaks.

Charles watched the helicopter pass overhead, but a man like Johan Krauss did not concern him. A rich and devious man, Krauss was, first and foremost, a businessman, unlike the other men interested in taking up residence on the islands. *Let him arrive first. It will only make his death all the sweeter,* Charles thought as the helicopter disappeared behind the island.

Having studied the satellite photos, Charles knew that the north side of the island offered a somewhat hidden bay, set between the rocky cliffs that formed the northern shore. It offered the perfect place to make land, because nobody would expect them to come from that direction.

The Swedes would almost certainly go for the long beaches of the southern and eastern walls. Not that they were a threat. Even less so than Krauss. The Swedes were just after the money, looking to claim the land simply to take a payday for leaving it again.

"Remember, anybody else on this island is a fair target, but shoot at nothing, and I will cut your balls off and hang them from the railings of my boat," Charles growled as the small landing party prepared to disembark.

The seven man, five mercenaries, Charles and Eamon, looked almost comical in the two dinghy's take took them from boat to shore.

"Keep together. I want us to move around this hill and claim the beach. We will meet the Swedes as they land. Hunting Krauss down will be fun," Charles spoke to the group.

"What if he flies away?" Eamon asked.

"Well, that is where you come in, Eamon. You still have that thing I gave you before we left?" Charles responded, turning to address his friend.

"Oh, yes, I do. I do have it," Eamon said, reaching back into the boat. He picked up a handheld RPG.

"Great. If that chopper takes to the sky, for any reason, I want you to handle it for me." Charles laid his hand on his friend's muscular shoulder.

"Alright, Charles." Eamon smiled.

"Get a bit closer and you can lick his asshole, Tiny," one of the mercenaries spat, much to the amusement of the others.

Charles moved like the wind, driving a balled-up fist into the gut of the laughing hired gun. The man doubled over, coughing and choking. He collapsed to his knees, gasping for air.

Charles grabbed the man by the throat, squeezing harder and harder until his frantic gasps for breath fell to a reasonable level. "One more word like that about my friend, my brother, and I will rip out your tongue and shove it up your asshole. Do you understand me, you prick?"

The man could not answer, the grip on his throat too tight to allow anything but a gurgled whistle to escape his lips.

"Good." Charles let go, and the man fell to the floor.

Nobody said anything, they simply fell into formation and set off around the base of the mountain.

The heat beat down on them, and the density of the vegetation worked against them every step of the way. The muddy ground seemed to suck at their feet, while a patch of vines, with thorns as long as fingers, held them up also.

They took turns in hacking a path through the dense foliage, two men leading the group, while they others held back, conserving their energy.

They made no attempts to remain quiet, grunting, shouting, and cursing. They feared nothing, and wanted people to know they were coming.

None of them heard the rustling of vegetation, as the hunters moved in.

"We are almost through," one of the mercenaries said, as he walked back to take his rest. He was a burly man whose face was a deep red even when not exerting himself in the jungle. His thick muscular arms were covered in tattoos. He crouched down and took a drink of water before announcing. "I need to take a piss."

He walked away into the trees, his figure disappearing completely the moment he left the trail they had cut.

Peter unzipped, farted, and soon a thick stream of steaming piss hit the ground, splashing off the leaves and plants as it went.

Behind him, something moved.

"Oi, if you want to see my cock, you can just ask, you little bitch," he snarled over his shoulder.

Nobody answered, but the trees to his left rustled, and a twig snapped.

Peter had a pistol on his hip. Stopping the flow, he grabbed his gun and turned around.

A large orange eye stared at him from the trees. The head appeared, pushing aside the plants. The grey-brown skin and thick snout led on to open jaws, displaying razor-sharp teeth. The creature tilted its head as it regarded Peter.

It gave a growl, a deep resonating rumble. Behind him, Peter heard the trees move. To his left, another face appeared. The creatures closed in.

The flow reopened, and strong smelling urine stained Peter's trousers.

His gun-wielding hand trembled. He tried to raise it, to at last make a stand, but it was useless. They moved too fast.

They attacked in a wave, moving forward to strike, before darting back again. The first slash came from the rear. Pain exploded in Peter's head as the sharp claws split the skin down his spine. Before he knew it, the second moved in, powerful jaws snapping at his arm, tearing it from his body in a single effortless snap. Peter opened his mouth to scream, but shock engulfed him. He could not speak; he could not move.

Slowly, the third creature emerged from the trees. At least five meters long, it stood up, rising above Peter, whose bowels emptied. He felt the warm stream of liquid shit travel down his legs, where it mingled on the floor with the deepening pool of blood, mud, and piss.

The creature observed Peter, a strange ticking sound repeating in his throat, steady and rhythmic. It reached forward, a long, curled claw unfurling. It stroked Peter across the chest; the touch was gentle and terrifying.

Peter's entire body trembled as the claw traced a path up his chest onto his face, running along the contours of his chin. He could hear the sharp edge drag over his skin like a dry razor. He swallowed hard and the creature flinched.

Lowering its head, the creature snorted in Peter's face. The exhalation was forceful, and the sour stench of its breath made Peter gag.

The beast jerked its arm, and the claw sliced open Peter's stomach. A rush of blood cascaded to the floor, pulling his internal organs with it.

Peter sank to his knees, trapping a thick strand of sausage-like intestine beneath him, sending even more of his innards hurtling to the floor.

Peter had no chance to warn the others. The three beasts moved on, leaving him to drown in a pool of his own making. In his final moments, Peter thought about praying, but a large raptor foot squashed his head like a grape before he could start.

The attack happened fast. The beasts broke through the trees with a jump. The shocked group spun around, reaching for their weapons. The two closest mercenaries were decapitated before their eyes could register the identity of the death-dealing creatures.

Large powerful jaws snapped shut, wrenching skulls from bodies in a shower of hot blood. Further back, Captain Droz, the leader of the mercenary force, pulled the trigger on his automatic rifle, firing a long, sustained burst into the chest of the nearest creature. Its lizard-like skin tore open, and blood poured from the fist-sized hole the bullets managed to create.

Rather than go down, however, the creature gave a roar and leaped towards Droz. Landing atop the man, the beast pinned him to the floor, large hooked talons spearing through his shoulders and into the soft ground beneath.

Droz cried out in pain as the creature tore into him with short front arms, flaying his skin in a frenzied attack before succumbing to its injuries. Collapsing forward, the beast crushed Droz beneath it.

The two remaining creatures saw the demise of their brother and turned in unison to the remaining three members of the group. One mercenary emptied the clip of his rifle in a spray of bullets that went high and wide, not even threatening to touch the dinosaurs that stood before him.

Switching for the smaller firearm on his hip, raised it, and pulled the trigger. His head exploded in a puff of skull fragments and globs of steaming brain matter.

"Eamon, forget about the helicopter, fire at them," Charles said as he turned to run, leaving his friend, his brother, to fend for himself.

For the first time in his life, Eamon did not stop to think about an order. He understood it immediately and raised the RPG to his shoulder. The two creatures stared at him, their heads cocked inquisitively.

Eamon pulled the trigger and the world around him shuddered. The rocket flew from the launcher, the force of it making Eamon's knees buckle.

One of the raptors moved, lunging forwards, its body dipping beneath the projectile. On his knees, Eamon watched as the remaining creature was blown to pieces by the rocket. The explosion tore the plants from the ground and sent a fireball barrelling into the sky. Charred raptor flesh rained down around them, while in the crater left behind, all that remained of the beast was a flowered lump of charred flesh and a foot stump. The skull landed with a thud not far from where Eamon lay, pinned beneath the bulk of the third raptor, whose long claws had effortlessly disembowelled the man.

"Char … Charles," Eamon coughed, blood bubbling from his mouth. He craned his head to look for his friend but found he was all alone.

The raptor took off through the trees, leaving Eamon to die with his guts in his hands.

Charles forced his way through the spiny plants. Long thorns tore chunks from his flesh, ripping his arms and face apart, but his fear kept him moving.

He could hear the creature behind him but knew that if he could make it through the dense vegetation, he stood a chance.

Charles burst through the bush and into a clearing. He spun as he broke free, his rifle raised ready to fire at the creatures in pursuit. Blood blurred his vision, and his left hand was close to useless, the flesh all but removed from the back of his hand and along his forearm.

"Come on, you son of a bitch," Charles growled, waiting.

He never heard the fourth raptor until it was too late. He turned and fired a burst, but the rifle fell to the floor before the last round was discharged. With a wet snack and a crisp crunch of bone being ground by powerful jaws, Charles headless body fell to the jungle floor.

The pursuing raptor appeared through the trees, its flank scorched and raw from the rocket detonation. The two creatures looked at each other for a moment, and then together they tore Charles's body apart.

CHAPTER 2

"Did you hear that?" Godfrey said as he and Johan slid into the helicopter.

"I did. I think our friend Mr. Gallway finally met his match," Johan said with a smile.

"What do you mean?" Godfrey asked, no longer interested in keeping his fear hidden.

"Godfrey, you do not think I would simply come to these islands blind, do you? I have had a small team checking the land within days of receiving the tip of its existence." Johan smiled, and when he did, his eyes twinkled with a naughtiness that had been there since he was a toddler.

"Who? I don't understand, boss," Godfrey said as he flicked the rotors into life.

"I sent a team of hired hands out here the moment I heard about this islands location. They sent me several reports back before … well, before the island got them." The smile returned, only this time, the face behind it looked maniacal.

"I think we can head back to the coast now, Godfrey. We have nothing to fear, and I have accomplished what I came for. The islands ae mine." Johan pulled his door closed and put the headphones over his ears without saying another word.

As the chopper took to the skies, another boat came into view, heading straight for the large bay on the northern side of the island.

"Oh, I don't think we need to worry about them, Godfrey," Johan said, not even bothering to look down at the Swedish boat, or the large shadow that moved through the water beneath it.

***

Karl Johnson stood behind the control of his yacht. A rich man, he liked to take control of his own operations. There were a lot of people in the world who would want to see him dead, and leaving his fate in the hands of anybody but himself seemed ludicrous to him.

11

His crew, a combination of family and close friends, held his closest of confidences. The islands were going to be his opportunity at taking things to a new level. With three islands at his disposal, he would finally be able to create the fortress he needed; a place of solitude, where he could sleep soundly once more. His hold on the Scandinavian drug trade was concrete, and the new land mass would allow him to take control of production as well as supply.

The waters were smooth, and as Karl looked at the main island looming large before him and the long thin third island in the distance, he saw nothing but money.

It would be a change. His wife and kids would need to adjust to the new location, but boarding school would take care of the kids, and well, if his wife did not want to come, there were plenty of others who would.

"Lukas, Viktor," Karl called down to his brothers. "We are coming up on the island. I want you out there watching for anything in the water. I trust your eyes better than any equipment on this thing."

Lukas and Viktor were younger than Karl, but both eminently larger in all proportions. Lukas was a mountain of muscle, a veritable giant of a man who, with his blond hair and blue eyes, looked every bit the Viking. Viktor was similarly large, but his muscle was also accompanied by a large gut from years of bad diet and Viking quantities of beer.

Each man moved around to the front of the yacht, assuming a position either side of the bow's tip. They stood watching the water, looking for any rocks or other such submerged hazard.

Karl had not even told his family about the islands, not until after they set out to claim them. His paranoia was growing, and his circle of trusted ears reduced with each passing month.

"Did you hear that?" Viktor asked as a rumble ran through the air.

"It was just a noise, baby brother," Lukas answered with a smile.

"No, the islands, they are mad at us," Viktor said, his eyes leaving the water to stare at the tall mountains of the main island. "There is something off about these lands. I can feel it."

Lukas was silent, his own eyes scanning the deep greens and luscious foliage that began as soon as the beach ended. As the boat rounded the point of the island, he thought he caught sight of something darting through the trees. Squinting, he searched, but saw nothing.

Shaking his head, he turned to his brother. "Your crazy imagination is infectious, brother." Lukas smiled, bellowing a laugh that seemed to echo around them, even with the distance between the two islands.

Nearby, something splashed in the water. The sound rolled like an explosion. Both brothers looked at each other. While Lukas would never admit it, he had a bad feeling growing in his stomach.

He turned his head and looked up at the wheelhouse. He could not see anything because of the sun glinting on the dark-tinted windows, but he knew his brother would be watching them.

"Stay alert, Viktor, Karl is always watching," he whispered, shuddering as the thought of his brother's disappointment tickled the back of his neck.

Both men feared their brother. They were there when he murdered their father in cold blood, executing him in order to take control of the family business. While neither would deny the change in business practices led to increased wealth, the knowledge of how it happened haunted both their dreams.

Without warning, the boat lurched suddenly to starboard. Both brothers stood off balance, and as a result, the impact threw them to the floor.

"What was that?" Viktor asked, pulling himself to his feet.

"*Idioter*," Karl roared in Swedish, his temper racing down the boat ahead of the rest of him.

"I don't see any rocks," Viktor spoke, hurried, calling up to his captain, hoping to hold him at bay.

"The water is clear," Lukas called immediately

Both men held their breath while the rest of the crew wore similarly pensive expressions.

The second impact hit the boat from underneath, lifting it clean from the water, before dropping it back down. Men cried out as their bodies broke and snapped from the jarring return to earth. The sheer bulk of the two Johnson brothers kept them on their feet.

"What was that?" The question was repeated, voiced by almost everybody still able to speak.

"Look, in the water." Viktor pointed.

The shadow disappeared in an instant, the creature below the surface surged upward, breaking the surface, towering above the Swedish yacht before it came crashing down.

At least fifty feet long, the creature bore no resemblance to any beast people had seen before.

"A sea monster."

"It's the Kraken."

"Turn us around, Karl, turn us around," a crewmember screamed.

Cries rang out as everybody panicked and yelled over one another. Both Viktor and Lukas appeared on the main deck, just as Karl came down the steps from the wheelhouse.

"Did you see that beast, brother?" Viktor asked.

Karl did not reply, but shot his youngest brother a look at made his blood run cold.

"Karl, Karl, we need to turn this boat around. That thing will kill us all," Axel, a cousin to the brothers, called.

"Nonsense, Axel. Surely you have seen a whale breaching before," Karl began.

"Karl, that was no whale," Axel interrupted, before a gunshot silenced him.

"If I say that was a whale, then it was a whale, and you will do better than to contradict me," Karl shouted as Axel's body hit the deck. "Now I want everybody in their places. We are bringing this boat ashore. I want these motherfucking islands. Are we clear?"

Nobody dared answer Karl, or even hold eye contact with him. Silence indicated agreement on a Johnson vessel.

"Good." Turning, Karl climbed back up to the wheelhouse.

People assumed their positions again. The sea was calm, sparkling in the sun. After several minutes of silence, the crew began to believe that they had indeed been spooked by a whale.

They relaxed, and a nervous chatter broke out. Then the creature struck once more.

Rising up from the rear of the yacht, many did not even see the attack coming. The giant crocodile-like head, with jaws the size of a station wagon, surged out of the ocean. The crashing wave of water wiped many off their feet, and as the enormous body twisted, the jaws closed, sweeping the deck clear. Half of the crew was gone in an instant, swallowed whole.

The deck of the yacht was a wreck as the gargantuan body slid back into the water. Fixtures and fittings, everything had been torn free. The deck battered, a gaping hole of obliterated fiberglass consuming the majority of its surface.

Three men remained on the deck, their weapons raised, trembling in their hands. They twisted and turned, scanning the water for signs of the monster. From behind them, on the island, a roar rang out which, even from a distance, make the air tremble.

"Where is it?" Viktor and Lukas appeared again, both men perspiring from their bout of cardiovascular exertion.

"I don't know," Walter, the only non-blood family member on the boat, spoke up. He turned around, his face pale with fear, a fact that only served to terrify the two brothers.

Their sister had insisted that Karl bring Walter on board. Anna was the one person in the world not afraid of Karl. She told them of her husband's history, and to that day, he had lived up to ever fabled tale of his exploits. To see him fearful was to see disbelief on the face of a God.

"Karl," Viktor called out, unable to finish his sentence because of the rushing water that consumed him.

The creature rose from beneath the boat, its body hitting like a torpedo, tearing the hull in two.

Its body was round and fishlike. The large scales, each at least twelve inches across, looked more like armoured plates. Large fore-fins slapped against the boat, fully separating the two halves from one another.

Viktor was lost, his body thrown by the initial upwards blow. Above them, Karl called out as he was thrown from the wheelhouse. He fell on the broken deck, his body landing with the sickening snap of breaking bones. A large shard of hull speared through the back of his head, forcing both eyes from their sockets, leaving them dangling either side of his skull. His body twitched, fighting to the last moment.

The beast was gone again, disappearing below the waves, its long spiny tail thrashing against the sinking boat as it dove beneath the water. One thrash caught Walter, crushing his chest, and throwing him against the wall. He fell to the floor, dead, leaving Lukas alone.

Jumping from the wreckage, he dove into the water and started swimming. Panic consumed him, direction lost all meaning and importance. Distance from the sinking ship was his only concern. Misguided as it was, his survival instinct merely told him to flee one situation. The rest would come later.

Lukas swam, pulling his giant body through the water with long powerful thrusts. With each stroke, he imagined the jaws closing around him, darkness was his future. He cried and shouted as every time he lived to swim a little further. He found it cruel, convinced the creature was toying with him.

When his feet first hit solid ground beneath the waves, he did not believe it.

Exhausted, crawling and clawing his way up onto the rocky shore, Lukas pulled himself from the water. The sharp rocks sliced into his hands, carving deep gouges into his flesh, but he did not care. Wounds would heal, and he had survived worse in his years.

Collapsing on his back, Lukas took deep gulps of air. He could not move. His vision blurred, moving from bright to dim, sharp-edged to a blur. He fought to remain conscious. He knew he needed to keep moving.

To his right, something moved. He heard a rustling, clicking, clacking noise. It made him think of the scurrying sound cockroaches made when chased.

Turning his head, Lukas opened his mouth to scream as the large, flat-bodied roach-like creature walked toward him. Squatting down, it smothered him, while pincers tore the flesh from his face.

Lukas screamed until his throat was mercifully torn out with the wet rip of tearing cloth.

CHAPTER 3

The helicopters came in waves, bringing with them fresh rounds of supplies and crew members, both of which were used up at an alarming rate.

Construction work on had been going on for almost three months, and in that time, seventeen crew members had disappeared. They strayed from the guarded complex and were never heard from again. People knew better than to ask. They were paid too much to care.

They all heard the roars that came from the trees, and there were stories depicting monsters of all shapes and sizes, but nobody pressed the matter. Such tales were written off as scaremongering tactics, designed to keep people working and on site at all times.

The contracts each man signed were simple and specific. Each crew member would be paid fifty-thousand dollars in cash money, with an additional bonus payment for completing everything on time. The only requirements were complete segregation; you arrived on the island, and worked on the island until the job was done, and you did not ask questions.

Orders were given from one of three identified Black Arrow Security operatives, and they were to be followed to the letter. Anybody failing to meet those requirements would be removed from the site and their pay forfeited.

"With fear and money, you can control the world," Johan said as he lit the Cuban cigar he held clenched between his teeth. They stood on the top floor of the rapidly constructed main building on the central island. Named by those that worked there as Hot Pocket, after the active volcano that provided the highest point on the island.

The building had four floors and was built on the rocky plateau Johan had first found four months previously. A tropical storm had kept them from moving in to commence construction for almost a month.

Johan Krauss was the Owner and CEO of Black Arrow Security, a privately contracted firm who had strong connections to several political leaders and nations. Their reputation was one tainted with accusations of the role they had played in both the War on Iraq, Afghanistan, Syria, and even the recent assassination of the Turkish president.

The company's name was clean. None of the charges raised ever stuck. Black Arrow never left a paper trail. Krauss saw to it that those sorts of things were taken care of.

The island facility was a gold mine for him. The finder's fee alone was astronomical. Black Arrow moved in first and established a well-guarded perimeter. They built reinforced walls that kept the local wildlife away from the contraction sites, and had patrols on the sentry posts twenty-four hours a day.

It was a costly operation, but one that Johan knew was necessary. The plans for the island were drawn up, and Johan saw to it that the people brought in to work on the project were capable to work under the presented condition, and more importantly, expendable, because accidents happen, and questions are a man's worst enemy.

In the distance, a roar shattered the silence of the night. Below him, the workers scurried back to their tents and shelters. The island terrified them, as it rightly should. For large periods of the day, that fact could be forgotten, at least forced into the recesses of the mind, as work took center stage.

Only when the work was done, the shifts ended, and the night rolled in, did fear once again raise its head, creeping out into the darkness like some nocturnal beast, waking and stretching before running rampant through the minds of those left behind.

The roar was enough to send them running for shelter, for even the thin canvas of their tents and the synthetic sleeping bags and bed covers meant an extra layer between them and the beast. While not much, it was all they had, and they learned to be grateful for it.

"They cry, you know," Amare said as he moved beside Johan.

Amare had worked for Black Arrow for over twenty years. In that time, he had worked his way up from a skinny kid who stumbled into the wrong place at the wrong time, to the head of security. He was a grizzled thirty-year-old man, with a strong body, skin as black as a void in space, and the coldest blue eyes Johan had ever seen.

There was nobody besides Godfrey who Johan trusted more.

"I remember you used to cry in your sleep too, Amare," Johan answered without looking round.

The man said nothing. "They are afraid of the creatures on this island. It makes them work hard." The African man laughed at the weakness of the men below him.

"We are making good progress. I say, let them stay afraid. If needed, make sure they remember that fear every now and then," Johan said, turning slowly to face his head of security. "You are a trusted friend, Amare, I know you will do right by this place."

The African man said nothing, but closed his eyes and bowed his head.

"I need to leave now. I have a meeting tomorrow with the men whose idea this is. I will be back, and until then, I trust you to keep progress moving. Any means necessary, Amare. You have my full support." Johan walked away, knowing the man would not give an answer. It was not his way to accept praise.

Johan remembered the first week after Amare's arrival, all those years ago. The group had been taunting Amare. He was small, a child, who claimed to be ten years old, but looked no bigger than seven or eight. They teased him for being small, for being a baby. They were all sixteen, juiced up on hormones and the thrill of holding real guns.

It had been an early mission for the fledgling Black Arrow Security, a trial run of sorts with the Congolese government. No questions asked.

One afternoon, the boys set on Amare, beating him with sticks and stones until he was bleeding and weeping on the floor. Johan took pity on the boy, carrying him into his own home, to tend to his wounds.

That night, Amara strode into the boys' tent and slit the throats of the two biggest members of the group. He sat by the bodies until the following morning, just to hear the screams of the others as they saw what he had done.

Johan arrived and stared at the scene, and stared into Amare's eyes. The cold blue eyes of a boy who had become a man ahead of his time. A man who would kill anything that stood before him. Johan nodded at the boy, who rose to his feet, and walked through the group of boys, who leaped from his path, towards him. Stopping, he dropped to one knee, pulled a knife from the belt of his trousers and swiftly sliced off the ring finger on his left hand, severing it at the palm. He did not cry, he made no sound. Rising, Amare presented the bloodied digit to Johan, and walked away. A token of loyalty, Amare swore himself to servitude, and in all the years, and all the battles since, his loyalty had not once come into question.

Godfrey stood waiting for his boss by the helicopter. His dislike of the island grew more with each visit he made. The knowledge of what lived in the trees terrified him. Unlike many of the men who worked for Black Arrow, he was not from a military background. His skills were not so much combat ready but rather specific to guarding an individual. A fighter by trade, he competed in bare knuckle boxing fights in the back streets of London, and any other city that offered him enough cash to turn up and dish out the pain.

He moved into MMA before it became mainstream, and honed his skills by beating men one on one. Time had proven him to be equally effective in situations up to three on one. Four was too many, and on winter mornings, his jaw would lock and remind him of the beating he had taken in Wolverhampton. Ironically enough, it had been as he stumbled out of the alleyway, blood pouring from his shattered mouth, the teeth he could find clenched in his fist, that Godfrey first met Johan.

A limousine pulled to the curb, in front of a stumbling and bloodied Godfrey. Doors had opened, and strong hands took hold, throwing him into the back of the stretched car. Godfrey woke in a hospital bed in a private ward. His injuries had been taken care of, and when his reconstructed jaw was healed, he also received new teeth.

His loyalty to Johan was born from a debt that he vowed to repay, but now it was something else. It ran deeper than blood in Godfrey's mind.

"You will be happy to hear, we can leave, Godfrey," Johan called as he walked up to the chopper.

"Very good, sir," Godfrey said, trying hard to hide his relief.

CHAPTER 4

"Joe, Joe, are you awake?" Pete Hawthorn shook his bunk mate by the shoulder.

"What, what time is it?" Joe muttered, rolling over, turning his back on his friend.

The pair went way back to their school days, or rather the days they should have been in school, and not messing around on the streets, causing more trouble than was good for them.

"Wake up, dude. It's time. If we are going to do this, we have to do it now. The watch is changing, and I can't take another day of this," Pete said, shaking his friend harder. Yanking the covers off the bed, he punched his friend as hard as he could on the arm.

"Hey—" Joe cried out, but his friend's hand smothered his mouth.

"Shhhh, don't wake them. We need to move, now," Pete whispered, speaking slowly.

The fog of sleep cleared from his mind and he nodded his head, understanding dawning on him.

Joe jumped from the top bunk, landing quietly on his feet. The pair each pulled out a bag they had pre-packed with clothes and supplies, scraps of food they had saved up from the previous days; enough to keep them going through the heat of the following day.

The two men crept through the tent, stepping over the sleeping bodies, not that anybody would have noticed the men had they woken, or even cared had recognition been achieved. Cramped together in tight lodgings, the humidity of the night soon became unbearable for most. Sojourns outside to cool off or simply to use the primitive facilities were more than common.

The friends made it outside without disturbing anybody. Both were light on their feet, a trait one learned quickly on the streets. Their grace was never what lead to them getting caught. Their slow brains and limited capacity for independent thought when in the presence of an alpha male character were what proved to be their downfall, time and time again.

"Where to?" Joe asked Pete, whispering in the dark.

The darkness was near total. The only illumination came from the stars, which, while in their multitude, never seemed to be strong enough to provide much more than a slight dent in the density of the dark. The moon had long since disappeared behind the volcano, another reason why the timing of their escape needed to be so precise.

"Wait here, the shifts will change in two minutes. That gives us some time to climb the wall over on the east side. We can make it up and over before the new crew takes position. We should be good. Stay quiet, make our way down to the water. We can swim to the first island and wait for the supply boats to come along. We sneak on board, hide down below decks, and ride that son of a bitch all the way to the end." Pete smiled at himself. The plan was an item entirely of his own creation, and he believed it to be his finest yet.

"That's a lot of work, Pete," Joe yawned.

"Well, you want to stay here even longer? Crammed in like sheep, sent to the slaughter for working too well, or not well enough. Fuck that shit, dude. I'm done." Pete raised his head. He could hear the chatter of the guards. "Shit, we missed it. Come on, leg it."

Pushing his friend, who moved more through fear of being discovered than his wholehearted belief in their plan, Pete ran for the fence.

The guards' voices grew louder as they marched through the sleeping construction workers to the somewhat more luxurious quarters reserved for the security force.

"Hurry, man," Pete growled as they reached the wall. Starting his climb, he hauled himself up to the top, threw over his left leg and sat, looking down at his friend. "Come on, Joe."

Joe made slow progress on the climb. Twice, he lost his footing and almost fell. Guards passed them by, too close for comfort, but too absorbed in their own complaints to notice the escape attempt.

Reaching down, Pete offered his hand to his friend and hauled his body up and over the wall.

"That was harder than it looked," Joe said, rubbing at his wrist. "Think I broke my damn arm."

Together, the men swung their bodies over the wall and dropped down to the ground the other side.

"Jesus fuck." Pete bit his tongue, swallowing the pained roar that built in his throat.

The drop had been high, fifteen feet on the lowest section of the wall, and made worse by the terrain on the other side, which consisted of rocks and bare earth, piled up in a form of barricade against the wall itself.

Pete's foot twisted beneath him as he landed. Both men heard the snapping sound of bones and tendons being forced to move in ways they were not designed to do.

"Are you alright?" Joe asked sheepishly.

"Right as fucking rain, mate." Pete grimaced. "Help me up, we need to keep moving."

Fighting back the tears, his jaw clenched to the point of cramp, Pete limped his way towards the trees. The rocky terrain beneath them soon gave way to soft grass, a large expanse that extended out towards the woods. Stumps poked from the ground to show where the area had been cleared. No doubt to give the guards more warning should anything living in the trees decide to attack.

"We made it," Joe said, falling into the tall grass, collapsing under the strain of carrying his friend.

The labour camp conditions of the builds came had stripped Pete of the blubber he had been carrying ever since the first day of high school, but it had already reduced their physical wellbeing by a similar margin.

Both men were spent, and their trek had only just begun.

"Can we rest?" Joe asked.

"Sure, but just a minute. We need to keep moving. The supply boat will arrive tomorrow. I want to get off this island as soon as possible," Pete answered.

"Did you hear that?" Joe said, snapping into consciousness. He had started drifting off to sleep.

Something rustled in the tall grass behind them.

"Pete, Pete, wake up. Did you hear that?" Joe nudged his friend with his elbow.

"Hear what?" Pete asked. A few moments later, the realization of their nap, however short, dawned on Pete, and he jolted into a sitting position. The result was a sweeping wave of pain radiating from his ankle, which burned as if trapped in a fire.

The rustling sound came again, closer this time.

"That," Joe said, getting to his feet.

"Help me up," Pete said, holding out an arm.

In the next moment, a fresh wave of pain engulfed him. Recoiling, Pete just managed to hold in his scream. Withdrawing his arm, he saw that three fingers of his left hand had been removed. The blood glistened in the darkness.

Shock powered Pete to his feet. He spun around, panic consuming him. He looked for Joe, catching sight of his friend running off into the trees.

The grass rustled again and Pete turned to face his attacker, giving himself just enough time to move out of the way. His leg wanted to buckle, but he held firm. The creature, which looked like some form of bipedal iguana, leaped through the air, snapping at Pete as it soared passed.

The thing landed in the grass with the soft thud, hidden from view by the knee-high vegetation. Pete turned to run. Three more creatures jumped up. One latched onto his face, sharp claws hooked into his cheeks, digging into his flesh as the creature scrambled for purchase. A claw found his left eye, the ball popping like a liquid-filled candy.

Pete screamed, unable to contain his agony any longer. The creature on his face scaled his body and stood perched on his head. Powerful claws in its rear legs had burrowed into Pete's skull, giving it a solid base.

The other creatures were also on him, climbing over him like over-eager kittens at play.

They tore chunks of flesh from his body, the result of their movements as well as their inquisitive bites. Their weight and the wounds they inflicted drove Pete to his knees. More appeared, smaller ones; children. They ran around him in circles, waiting for him to fall.

"Help me," Pete roared, hearing the clamour of the guards as they reacted to his screams.

The spotlight came on. Each guard post had a powerful spotlight mounted onto a pivot so that they could be aimed both inside as well as outside the camp walls.

The light was intense. It drove the creatures back into the cover of the grass. The light blinded Pete, who, still on his knees faced the camp.

"Help me, please," he cried, raising his bloodied arms to shield his eyes.

Joe saw the things in the grass, and he ran. He left his friend behind and ran, self-preservation being the most important aspect of his life.

From within the cover of the forest, his back pressed hard against the thick truck of a tall tree, he stood panting. Sweat slicked his flesh, and his legs shook from a mixture of shock, fading adrenaline and general exertion.

With his eyes closed, Joe listened for the sound of his pursuers. He heard Pete calling, he heard his best friend's screams, and he wept. Crying not only for his friend, but because of his cowardice. The gunshot brought him to attention. He froze, waiting for another. Maybe the guards were coming for them, clearing a path through whatever it was that truly lived in the woods.

No more sounds followed. Realization dawned on him as to what the gunshot signified. Joe swallowed, his mouth suddenly dry.

Joe needed to move. He needed to keep going, head to the coast and follow through with the plan. It was what Pete would have wanted.

Pushing off from the tree, casting himself into the total darkness of the forest, Joe began to move.

He took small shuffling steps, afraid that if his movements became too bold, he would trip and stumble.

The forest floor was thick with roots and vines, creeping plants and other vegetation. Fern leaves swatted at his face, with no clear, worn path to be found.

Something wrapped around Joe's feet. He tripped, stumbled, and fell. He landed face first, with a wet splat. The overpowering aroma of ammonia and shit filled his world. It was all he could smell, and all he could taste.

Pushing himself to his feet, his head came free from the pile of still-warm shit with a wet sucking noise. Wiping his eyes, trying to clear his face, Joe stumbled and ran. Blinded, he held his hands out, vomiting as he walked.

He fell repeatedly, walking into trees and plants. Thorns tore deep burrows into his flesh, and his shins became a magnet for the rocks that seemed to sprout from the ground as if the island grew them like fungus.

Without warning, Joe was falling again. Not from a trip this time, but because there was no more ground beneath his feet.

Joe screamed as he fell, blind to the distance or what lay below him. Fear was total. It consumed him to the point where it did not matter where he was, or what fate befell him. He braced his body, only to relax his body, unable to prepare for the unknown.

He hit the ground a few moments later. The ground opened up and swallowed him. Rushing over him, the water was cold. The impact was a jolt to his entire body, and the gasp Joe made at the moment of impact could not be helped. Water rushed into his open mouth, filling his lungs. Coughing and choking, Joe fought and kicked his way to the surface.

A break in the trees allowed for a small burst of starlight to filter through, casting enough of a luminescence for him to make out his location. He had fallen from a cliff into a small pool. Swimming as best he could, the act being something Joe had never taken to, even as a child, he hauled himself to the edge, then heaved himself up and out of the water.

He lay on the muddy bank, breathing heavily. His entire body ached, but he did not know if it was through injury, or merely the trick of his mind. He tried to move. Everything responded as he instructed, and inch by inch, Joe made his way up the beach and away from the water.

The ground solidified beneath him, sloping on a steep incline. Joe didn't care. He rolled onto his hand and knees, and crawled his way up, hoping to reach the top of the cliff.

The slope stopped suddenly, the hard ground falling level. Joe tried to stand when his foot went through the ground and into the hollow space below.

Yanking his foot free, Joe looked down and realized that what he stood on was not a solid mass or the crest of a hill, but rather a mound of disturbed ground.

He heard the approaching charge before he caught sight of the bodies shimmering in the darkness. Turning, Joe saw he had no place to run. They were coming at him on all sides, their bodies a shimmering sea of blackness. Ants, giant ants, closed the ground in no time, the first wave charging at the interloper that had attacked their home.

They swarmed over Joe, who tried frantically to swat them away. Their two-inch-long bodies were crushed by his blows, but their strength was in numbers, and with every nibbling bite their hungry jaws made, more toxin was forced into Joe's system.

The hallucinations began immediately, colours and lights exploding in his vision, conjuring up creatures of nightmarish worlds: creatures with rotting limbs and raw, weeping bodies; creatures that put the beasts of the island to shame.

The fractured ground splintered beneath Joe's feet, and he fell into the ant's inner sanctum. He fell to the floor, where he was absorbed into the waiting flood of insects. They swarmed over him, and in him. Probing bodies forced their way deep into his flesh through every available entry point. They burst through his ears and burrowed into his head.

Joe's screams died down, suffocated by the insectile flood, long before his life was finally taken from him.

CHAPTER 5

Amare stood and watched from the shadows of the main tower. He watched the men slink across the campsite, and heard their cumbersome attempts at scaling the wall, making a note to scold the men who failed to notice them.

He was keen to see how far they got. Very few survived long. He thought of it as a game. Had he held anybody on the island in close enough confidence, he would have placed wagers on the man leaving. It made him think of his time in Iraq. They had teased locals with bottles of water. Filling some with vodka, and some with bleach. They would throw the bottles from the truck and take bets on who would drink from which. Those sessions made him a very rich man on the base. Then one pissant called Phelps leaked a video of their fun onto Facebook, and everything changed overnight.

Amare took care of Phelps, removing his tongue before he slit his throat. He still had the dried appendage in his box of trophies, dating back to the finger he removed from his own hand. The box was getting full. He kept promising himself he would upgrade to something larger, but it always slipped his mind.

When the first man fell victim to the small creatures in the long grass, Amare grew angry. He could not help feeling cheated by the cheap way the men threw away their lives.

Bringing his rifle to his shoulder, he took aim and waited. The man would call for help. All the cowards called for help. When he did, Amare would happily oblige.

The call came, and Amare smiled as he pulled the trigger, finding the satisfaction he sought in seeing the man's head explode.

The second man made it to the trees, almost impressing Amare with his attempts. His screams a few moments later ruined everything. Amare waited, but nothing more came. Turning his back on the forest, he pulled a cigarette from the pack he always kept in his pocket, lit it, and took a long, deep drag.

Coughing the smoke out in rings, he sat down, as the next soldier on shift climbed up to the tower to begin his watch.

"Evening," the man spoke.

Clarke, an Australian by birth, but not by nature, had worked for Black Arrow for seven years. Amare liked him well as well as anybody else in the camp. Clarke had a strong dislike for everything Australian, including the military he had served for so long. His views on the ever-increasing impact of politics and political correctness on the military extended well beyond his own country's borders, but the majority of his ranting monologues would always circle back to his homeland.

"Evening. We just lost two men over the wall. Both dead now," Amare answered, reeling off the facts and nothing more. A cold man, he played his cards close to his chest, unless his hand was being forced, which was something that rarely happened anymore. People soon learned how to deal with him, and he would not have it any other way.

"Pisser. Guess that means replacements," Clarke said, unable to hide the density of his accent.

"They were useless. Their loss would not be noticed," Amare replied, rising to make his way down to the floor.

"Not leaving me alone up here, are ya? I thought we could play a round or two of Two-Up," Clarke said, spinning an old rifle casing over his fingers.

"No, I hate that game. You cheat," Amare grunted.

"You can't cheat at Two-Up, mate. You just can't guess 'em right," Clarke called after the disappearing figure, whose dark skin hid him from the world before he even reached the bottom of the ladder.

Amare made his way across the courtyard to the Black Arrow housing complex. Climbing into bed, he fell into a deep and troubled sleep. The ghosts of the past always found him. No matter where he fled in the world, they would always be waiting.

CHAPTER 6

Construction on the central island, whose name of Hot Pocket had spread even to the Black Arrow crew, had progressed ahead of schedule. The fear driven into the workers had them all the more eager to complete the building, collect their wages, and head back home.

Amare watched the main building bloom into a finished project of modern technology. It was such an eyesore on the stunning visual landscape that was the island, that it became almost beautiful as a result.

Around them, the perimeter fence had been extended, and a more permanent, double-reinforced construction had taken its place; iron and concrete surrounded by a ceramic coating that offered enough protection to stop any modern missile from breaching the barrier. It also had a secondary element: a solar-fuelled electrical current. Anything that touched the fence from the outside was immediately hit with enough juice to barbeque a charging rhinoceros.

Within the walls, an artificial ground had been laid down, and four more buildings had been erected. In the process, the construction crews, who had since grown accustomed to the labour camp conditions that Amare sustained, were able to abandon their tents in favour of one of the permanent structures. A good thing too, for they discovered the island came with a storm season; hurricane-style winds, torrential rain, and thunderstorms that sounded more like the creatures from *War of the Worlds* descending to earth than anything else.

The temporary sleeping area was washed away the first night the men moved into the building, known only as Building C.

"Chalky, chalky do you read, over?" The twang of Clarke's Australian accent was unmistakable, even above the sound of the approaching storm.

"I told you not to call me that," Amare barked.

"Sorry, mate, gotta call ya something," Clarke offered in response.

"What do you want?" Amare had no interest in talking. He loved the storms and wanted to enjoy every moment of it.

"We just finished construction on the two sub joints out here. The weather is setting in, so I wouldn't risk sending anybody back your way, but when it clears, I reckon a single crew would be enough to finish off what we need," Clarke explained. It was clear to hear the bragging in his voice at having finished his section first.

Since the building work on the main structure had finished, the work had been split over the two remaining islands. Smaller complexes were created, with additional manpower being sent daily. On any other part of the planet, the scale of the operation being put into place would have been considered a marvel.

"Send them straight to the other island. I don't need them here, and they lost four men yesterday," Amare said, his eyes scanning the growing mound of paperwork on the table before him.

Not a record's keeper by nature, Amare could not pinpoint the time he fell into the bad habit. Paperwork meant a paper trail, and paper trails could be followed.

"Alright, mate. Good call. Anyway, the storm is really starting to set in. It'll be silence from us until it's over. The big guy is visiting in the next clear patch, so we should make sure we push these guys for all they are worth. The end is in sight." While Clarke and Amare did not agree on a great many things, their dislike of the island was a shared facet of their lives.

Amare said nothing as the radio fell silent. He stood and walked from the room. Heading for the roof, he stood in the wind and listened to the storm build around him. He could feel its power and sought to energize himself through it.

With construction on the individual islands complete, the final stage of the project was able to begin. Interconnecting skywalks were built and heaved into place, connecting the three islands. Simple in their construction, the encapsulated suspension bridges were secured in place with carbon-fibre-reinforced polymer cables.

Johan stopped walking in the centre of the bridge that connected the main island with the long, thin, third island. The bridge had a gentle swing to it, but the fair weather that had set in since the storms abated made conditions for a final inspection near perfect.

"I am impressed, my friend," he said to Amare, who had accompanied Johan and Godfrey on the inspection of the complex.

"I never fail," Amare said. After all of the years, Amare had never understood the need for small talk and praise. He knew his place and did what was asked of him.

"I know that. You are a trusted confidant. That is why I want you to remain on this island." Johan turned to face the man he thought of as a son.

"To finish building, of course. It would be my honour, sir." Amare bowed his head.

"I know the island is not your favourite place. You are not a fan of the sea, but I need to have my best man on the job." Johan reached out and laid a hand on Amare's shoulder.

"I will not fail you." Amare stood tall.

"The construction crew will leave in three weeks. You and a group of men will remain behind, to oversee the island and ensure that everything runs according to plan. The bidding will take place on October fifteenth. Once that has happened, I would expect the rest to happen swiftly." Johan nodded as he spoke, his eyes once again returning to the sea. A large shadow passed beneath the water, travelling between the two islands, moving directly beneath their feet. "Once the money has been transferred, we will step back from the island, and leave it in the control of those that bought it. You stand to make a lot of money on this deal, Amare, and I am sure you will want to talk about your future when this is done."

Amare did not answer. He had no need for money, no interest in doing anything other than what he did. His bank balance was spread over seventeen different institutions in five countries. He did not even know the number that would be used to verbally enumerate his wealth.

Johan resumed walking, making his way back to the secondary island, where they had one final location to inspect.

The third island was long and thin, no more than half a mile across at its narrowest, which also served as its midpoint.

Two locations had been built, the crews moving about via helicopter, never straying from the compound that had been erected for them.

There was one building on the north side of the island and another on the south. One was designed to be the main control center; the security hub. The power and override controls for the defences of the archipelago were housed in the short, squat building. The ground-level floor sat atop a deep underground level where the main controls were located, along with a hidden bunker that offered a reduced but nonetheless effective laboratory space; a scientific fallout shelter of sorts. A secondary satellite telecommunication portal would supply an emergency transmission beacon should it be required.

The building on the lower level was an operations chamber, where the main security campus would be located. It was a two-level structure with a vertically extending viewing tower rising from the centre; it had the look of a lighthouse when viewed up close.

CCTV cameras were positioned around the islands, strategically placed by the Black Arrow team before as well as during the construction process. In total, there were almost one hundred cameras split between the three islands, with requirements for more to be added once the buildings were fully converted and furnished.

Once Johan, Godfrey, and Amare reached the third island, they took the lift down to the ground level. The building had nothing else to offer, being merely a grounding point for the bridge. An armed group of Black Arrow guards stood waiting for them, having confirmed that the path was clear. Quad bikes took them from to the northern and southern buildings. Once there, armed guards took the small group through the buildings pointing out the various features that had been requested.

"I am very impressed. Good job, good job," Johan repeated every few rooms.

He could smell the money, and knew that when the islands opened up for auction, all of the usual suspects would be interested in entering a bid. He looked forward to the North Korean offer. They had been looking for a new experimental land mass for some time, and the possibilities offered by the local wildlife would triple the asking price. Nobody else knew about the beasts that lived in the jungles; only his own men knew, and their silence had been arranged. The construction workers were also taken care of with that regard.

Johan had no plans to reveal his secret weapon too early. He would let the bidding war settle, and then throw it in the pot to sweeten the deal.

The sun was starting to disappear behind the volcano as they emerged from the southern building. The final stop on their tour of the islands.

"Godfrey, please give me a moment with Amare here. Prepare for our departure, this will not take long." Johan stared at Amare as he spoke, a slight smile gracing his aged face.

Amare had no idea how old Johan was, but he had a timeless presence about him. Amare did not believe in witchcraft, but if anybody was to convince him of its existence, it would be Johan.

They stood in silence inside the main building, waiting for Godfrey's footsteps to fade to an echo.

"You wanted to talk to me?" Amare said after a time.

"Yes, Amare, I did. I know that you are a man who sees the world differently. I have known about this since I first met you. That night you killed those men, and presented me your finger will always shine in my mind. As we reach the end of this project, I have been left to wonder about how we will organize the trips home for those that worked on the project. I think I will leave this in your capable hands, my friend. I am sure you will be able to work something out." As was their custom, Amare nodded and looked down at his feet, while Johan walked away.

CHAPTER 7

The team of operatives within Black Arrow Security, the real team, the core unit who knew the reality of the company and their role within it, understood the tasks they were given. They accepted them without explanation, sound in the knowledge that their actions would be correct.

Their skills extended beyond the tasks they performed on the island. On the final day of construction, as everything being tidied away, these men stood up, knowing the time had come for their actions to carry meaning.

Collecting the different crews, which had been split into groups and sub-groups, they ushered them into the main building so as to organize their payment and release. A helicopter arrived, ready to carry out the transport back to the large vessel that had been sent to bring them home.

For the first time in many months, a murmur and general air of excitement and optimism rolled over the island. Even the rumbling volcano and the shuddering crashes the forest made from time to time could not dent their spirits.

"Shift seven, shift seven, please come inside, you need to sign the paperwork for your payment remittance," Dave spoke up, shouting to be heard over the excited babble of the crew.

The men moved inside, and Dave counted each head to make sure everybody was present and accounted for. Once he was content, he closed to doors and addressed the segregated group.

"Follow me," he instructed, turning before they had the chance to voice their concerns. "We will organize your payment and you will be on your way."

Drawn on by the promise of payment, the sum being a life changing amount for almost all of the men on the crew, they followed like sheep.

Through the corridor, and down two flights of stairs, into the underground levels they themselves helped build.

Disquiet grew amongst them as they entered what looked like an unfinished area, moving through a pair of security card guarded set of double doors. Bare brick flooring led them through a bare brick-walled corridor and into a large bare room.

They filed in, none the wiser. A few questioned the smell, the tainted odour that fell heavy on the senses. Only as the doors closed, did panic set in, and by then, it was too late.

The first burst of machine gun fire took out the majority of the group, round after round peppering their flesh. Blood spurted into the air at all angles as bodies fell left, right, and centre.

Those that escaped the first burst hammered on the doors and scratched at the walls in their desperate search for freedom, all to no avail as the second volley of fire strafed across the room like a hose. No body was left unpenetrated, flesh split, punctured burned and scorched as hot lead left its damning mark.

When the gun smoke cleared, the aroma of fresh blood and lightly charred flesh filled the small room. The door opened on the opposite side of the wall, and Amare walked in. He moved around the pile of fresh corpses, checking for any survivors. He found one man at the back. He had been shot repeatedly but clung to life, coughing and drowning in his own blood. The man turned his head towards Amare, a pleading look set in his ever-fading eyes.

He opened his mouth to beg for help, but the blade opened his throat and stole his final moments before he had a chance to voice his plea.

Once satisfied everybody was dead, Amare signalled for the others to come. Four men walked into the room and began dragging out the bodies.

The remains were deposited on the ground beyond the walls, accessed via a steel reinforced security door built directly into the fence, connected to the main building via an underground tunnel. Designed as an escape route, its first usage as a death tunnel would forever stain the walls and taint the air.

Deposited beyond the walls, the bodies were soon removed, and the sounds of crunching bone would echo from within the trees.

On the other side of the building, a similar process was in full-swing, and the bodies were transported through the tunnel via quad bike and cart.

Amare held up his hands and signalled for the approaching bike to stop.

"The last two groups will need to go to the sea. You will take them, and dump them from the cliffs." He gave the order and walked away.

By the time the sun set on the island region, the only men remaining were the Black Arrow crew. Many slept fitfully, troubled by the weight of the innocent lives clutching at their consciences, trying to drag them down to hell. The only one who slept a deep and dreamless sleep was Amare. For the first time in many years, the monsters and ghosts of his past left him be.

CHAPTER 8

The streets of Hong Kong were as crowded and as dirty as Johan remembered them.

The sun had gone down and darkness reigned over the city. As he made his way through the side streets, moving through the closed market stalls, rats the size of cats and small dogs would scurry left and right around him. The pickings were always good. Their size was no marvel when one saw the offerings left behind. Not just scraps but entire supplies were dumped in the alleyways. Everything not sold at the end of the day was useless to the poor traders. They had no storage or means to keep it fresh, and so they left it behind, safe in the knowledge that between the rats and the poor, nothing would remain come morning.

Johan knew where he was going. The address for such dealings never changed, and the route he took had become ingrained into his memory over the years.

Behind him, Godfrey followed; his shadow, loyal and true as always. Godfrey was always different in Hong Kong. The city agreed with him in some deep and unknown way. He would smile and be more relaxed, yet never less vigilant while walking the streets. Johan was sure that, should he cut his friend loose from servitude, Godfrey would remain in this place for the rest of his days.

They moved from one alley to another, and approaching the Wan Chei district, they found the streets busier. Pimps and whores stood in alleys, deep in conversation about how the night would pan out.

They saw money change hands, handed over from dour-looking whores to greedy-eyed pimps, who turned their stock around and shoved them straight back out to market. They witnessed blows being delivered when women held back their earnings or offered less than had been expected of them. In one alley, a nasty-looking man with a crack pipe between his teeth bounced back and forth from one foot to the others, a bloody knife in his hands. He laughed at the weapon, holding it up to his face for inspection.

"Let them be, Godfrey. Our business here is important, and we cannot become side-tracked by the trivialities of life," Johan spoke to his bodyguard. He knew how badly the man took to abusers of women. He had seen, on more than on occasion, how forceful Godfrey could be when educating such heavy-handed barbarians.

Under most circumstances, he would leave his trusted guard to his own devices, allow him to work the issues out of his system. He recognized that Godfrey grew up with his fists as the tools for solving disagreements, and understood the fighter mentality. Today was different, however. Today, there could be no distraction.

"Yes, sir," Godfrey whispered, falling in beside his boss rather than behind.

"Tomorrow, you can roam the streets and do what you will. I have no business and will retire to my lodgings, but today, we have a job to do," Johan replied, offering the reward for good behaviour.

They turning into a narrow alleyway that ran between two different nightclubs. Stopping half way down behind a tattered door that had seen better days, Johan adjusted his jacket and knocked four times. One slow, two fast, and one slow. Stepping back, he waited patiently while on the inside, the preparations were beginning for his entry.

The door opened, and two large Asian men appeared. They wore fitted suits that barely contained their muscles. Wider than they were tall, both were armed with pistols and chests that looked like they could stop bullets.

"Tell Mr. Sato that Mr. Krauss has arrived," Johan addressed the two men without concern.

The men, who could have, and most likely were, twins, looked at each other. They did not speak, but nodded, as instructions were spoken to them via the covert earpieces they wore.

The men stepped either side of the door and offered Johan entry. They moved to block Godfrey's path, however, shoving him back into the alley when he tried to make his way through.

"It will be fine, Godfrey. It looks like you will get your night off after all." Johan's voice drifted from behind the dual masses of human flesh that completely hid the door from view.

Godfrey stood his ground, staring down the two men before him. They were large, but Godfrey had fought bigger men in his days. If push came to shove, he would fight to the last drop.

"Godfrey, this night is important. Trust me, I will be fine here. I will contact you when we are done." The two men disappeared, and the door closed before Godfrey could give an answer.

Alone in the night, Godfrey paced the alley for a while, before heading off into the Hong Kong night. He had a bee buzzing in his bonnet and he needed to find a release.

***

The building Johan entered was a false front. Set between the two night clubs, it was only as wide as the doorway that covered it. A flight of stairs began after a short hallway, leading down at a steep angle. Another corridor followed, leading on to a single, large room. A long oval table stood in the centre of the room. It would not have looked out of place in any corporate boardroom across the globe.

Twelve tall-backed leather chairs sat around the table. Eleven were already occupied. The dark lighting in the room was purposefully set so that the guests were shrouded by darkness, in the name of political discretion.

"You are late, Mr. Krauss," one of the men around the table spoke. His heavy, eastern European accent did little to keep his identity a secret.

"Yes, it would seem that even I cannot control the traffic," Johan replied with a smile. He would not allow anybody to gain the upper hand in conversation. "Besides, I think you will find what I have to offer will more than make up for my unintentional tardiness."

The voice fell silent, and the atmosphere in the room changed. Johan's arrival signified the time for banter had ended, and the serious business had begun.

Johan sat and pulled a series of satellite photographs out of his briefcase. He placed them on the table, and waited. He did not speak. He knew the power of words, but understood the importance of silence. Knowing when to speak was half of the battle, and Johan was a skilled warrior in that department.

One by one, the men around the table browsed through the photographs, each waiting their turn before they offered the pack to the man beside them.

It took fifteen minutes before the papers were returned to Johan.

"Construction on the islands has been completed. The main building is located on the central island, with sub-units spread across seven different locations in total. Each island connects to the main location via a high-tensile bridging system, eliminating the need for vehicular travel from one to the other," Johan said without emotion. Emotion lost you money in such instances.

"I see a large security perimeter, what sort of armaments can be accommodated?" an accentless voice asked from a shadowy area at the far end of the table.

"At the moment, there is nothing, but the structure will accommodate any mountable armaments that you feel may be required," Johan answered.

"These look like heavy-duty fortifications. That is strange for an isolated location, especially when put in by the contractors without a specific request," an Asian-lilted voice entered the conversation.

"Yes, the fortifications were a requirement of the building process. That is something we will cover later. However, I think now would be a good time for the first round of closed bids." Johan had no interest in drawing out the process. He was in charge, and he needed to keep people on their toes.

The first round of bids came in and a clear winner emerged. The idea behind the bidding, as Johan ran it, was that even he did not know or interact with the eventual winner. That way, he remained impartial and could still work with any of the other bidders on other projects, even if this venture would be enough to let him retire and hand Black Arrow Security over to a new boss.

Once the round of bids was over, a second round of photos was shown, these depicting the base itself, the buildings, the rooms, and the potential, thanks to various mock-ups raised by a computer hacker who owed his freedom and continued computer access to Johan.

This prompted a break in discussions so that the delegates could make the calls they needed to make, back to their home bases, either confirming funds or requesting an extension of the existing bid ceiling.

Johan took the time to venture into the empty club above them. He took a glass of water and a cigarette. He could not help but smile to himself. Things were going even better than he imagined.

***

It did not take Godfrey long before he found what he was looking for. A man of his peculiar tastes could always find solace in Hong Kong. The women there were a talented bunch and were able to give him what he needed.

He was a man of conflicting principles. He could not stand violence against women, and the mere thought of a man beating a woman was enough to make his blood boil. What happened while fucking, however, was a different story. He became a different animal once the red haze of lust descended over his vision.

He wrapped his hands around the woman's throat, squeezing just enough to make her squirm, grinding her crotch hard against his, forcing him to enter her deeper.

He could feel his body tense as his orgasm build, which caused him to squeeze harder, to twist his young host's hardened nipples until she cried out in an intoxicating mix or pleasure and pain.

Releasing his hold on her throat as she began to buck and thrash like a woman possessed, he increased the tempo of his thrusts. Driving his hips forwards to the point where his flesh slapped against hers with such force, it required him to hold her by the shoulders so as not to break contact.

He came with a growl, driving himself deep, revelling in the feel of his seed and her juices mixing. Nothing beat a bareback fuck, and throughout the world, the girls of Hong Kong were always happy to take it.

Standing up, leaving the girl sprawled on the cold damp ground, her body still trembling in post orgasmic bliss, he pulled the notes out of his wallet and handed to the girl. He never discussed the price. He paid handsomely for what he got, and the women never complained either.

Turning, he stepped over the battered body of her pimp, who lay in a pile of his own teeth.

Godfrey caught the man delivering a beating to a pretty young thing, whipping her with his belt, berating her for god knows what. The other girls had been next in line before Godfrey came in, fists flying.

Zipping his trousers, Godfrey gave the pimp a kick as he walked away.

Before he reached the end of the alleyway, he heard footsteps behind him. With a sigh, he turned, ready to fight, but not really in the mood. A hard fuck always calmed him down.

"Listen, I can't be bothered," he began, but stopped talking when he realized there was nobody there.

Turning, cursing himself for growing old, Godfrey began to move. Something ran behind him. Something fell, and something stung. A strange and sudden burn hit his neck and spread. Godfrey was unconscious before he hit the floor.

The three men emerged from the shadows, stepping into the light as if they materialized from the air. Two bent down and picked up Godfrey's unconscious form, while the other checked on the pimp and the girl. The scene was clear enough, even had they not watched the whole thing unfold.

Without saying a word to one another, they half-carried, half-dragged Godfrey's form to the waiting van at the end of the alley.

"This is Recovery Team Six, we have the first package. Repeat, we have the first package," one of the men spoke, pulling a radio out of his pocket as he climbed behind the wheel of the van.

***

The clean, crisp smell of the meeting room was a welcome respite from the stale air of the club. The aroma of drink, sweat, and other bodily excretions held a particular pungency, which seemed to develop a uniquely sickening substance during the quiet daylight hours.

Johan was the first one back in the meeting room. Taking his seat, he waited. The longer it took, the greater the scramble for money. He would gladly wait for that.

One by one, the men returned, taking their seats in the shrouded edge of the table.

Johan waited for everybody to be seated, the odour of cigarettes and sweat pervaded the previously sterile atmosphere. The first few were cracking already. The purse strings were too tight, or the interest not there. Their loss. Johan would sell to the highest bidder and walk away, just the way he liked it.

"So, gentlemen, I have reviewed the bids and think it is about time we upped the stakes a little. You see, there is more to these islands than meets the eye," he began.

A crash from somewhere outside brought everybody to their feet. Shouts and the rattle of gunfire echoed down the hallway. Somebody was trying to get in.

The sound of footsteps echoed down the corridor, and suddenly everybody around the table grew nervous. Not only Johan had been forced to abandon his bodyguard. Nobody in the room was armed. All eyes spun towards Johan. The scent of betrayal heavy in the enclosed space.

"I know nothing of this," he said just as the doors to the room opened.

There was a clacking sound as two small canisters were rolled into the room. The moved down either side of the table.

"Bugger," Johan said, moments before the metal casings burst open and a thick white gas filled the room.

The people seated around the table had no time to react. They had no means of escape.

The gas put them to sleep in a matter of moments. Johan fought it long enough to see the doors open and a group of men walk in. They wore full hazmat styles suits. For the first time in many years, Johan felt a jolt of fear run through him, and then there was nothing. He pitched forward, not even able to bring his hands up to brace his face-plant onto the table.

CHAPTER 9

Johan came to with a pounding head and a dry mouth. His lips were glued together with the sticky remains of deep sleep. His tongue seemed heavy and useless in his mouth.

He opened his eyes, but had already taken stock of the blindfold that covered his face. It was too early to move; he was not in the mood to face his attackers just yet.

Instead, he listened. The world around him was noisy, and it soon dawned on him what caused it all. A plane; he was in a plane. Whoever had broken into the Hong Kong meeting room was moving him somewhere else.

"I think he is awake," a heavy American voice spoke up.

A few moments later, the blindfold was ripped from Johan's face, and the bright lights of the plane's interior came on.

"It is a pleasure to see you again, Mr. Kraus," a familiar-sounding voice spoke.

"You know, if you wanted the island, you could have just turned up to the auction." Johan forced the words over his lips. The after-effects of the drugs they had used made his body sluggish and clunky.

"Where would be the fun in that? Besides, the US government does not need to attend such backwater meetings, and you know it," the voice replied, surly and arrogant.

Johan raised his head and looked around. The interior of the plane was familiar. He had closed many deals over the years in the very same beast.

Open plan in so far as seating, a single line of chairs ran along the righthand wall of the fuselage. At either end of the long body, a cluster of rich-coloured leather sofas were arranged in a friendly yet imposing formation.

A bar and open-plan area occupied the main body of the aircraft. It was there that the man talking to Johan stood. He held a glass of whiskey and ice in one hand and the cluster of photographs Johan had handed around the table in his other.

"Join me, we will have a drink and toast our new venture together." The man smiled and raised his glass in Johan's direction before taking a deep sip.

Reluctant, but left with very few other options, Johan got to his feet and moved to the bar.

His drink was already waiting for him. Vodka on the rocks. Picking up the glass, he stared at the contents before taking a drink. The liquid felt cool and godly in his parched mouth, becoming a warm reassuring burn as it travelled down his throat to his stomach.

"Where is Godfrey?" Johan asked, wanting to make sure his bodyguard was unharmed.

"He, much like the others, is unharmed. Well, those two angry chinse fellows from the door, they are not quite so good, but they were given a choice, and they made it."

"Where is he?" Johan repeated.

"He's here, on this plane. He's sleeping on the couch over there, and don't worry. He won't wake up until after this little bit of business of ours is over with," the man leaned in and smiled. "Your secret dealings are always safe with us."

"Fuck you," Johan growled.

"Only if you buy me dinner first," the man replied, his expression stern. Slowly, however, it started to change. A smile spread across his lips, and the intensity of his gaze fell awake. "It's good to see you again, old friend."

"Likewise," Johan said, standing to embrace the man he considered one of his oldest friends. "Did you really have to drug me? For a moment there, I feared the worst."

"I'm sorry about that, but we could not take any risks. You see, we need that island. We know everything there is to know about it, so don't play any games, Johan." The voice was friendly, but still business.

Director Werkhoven was an older man, similar in age to Krauss, yet neither would admit to being older than the other. They went way back, almost to their childhood years.

Johan had grown up in the US, and spent the majority of his time there, relaxing in the anonymity of the alias he had been given: a large house in the California hills with a stunning panoramic view of the ocean.

He did not play favourites with his negotiations, and over the years, his contacts within the US government and such, had left him to be. Only three times in recent memory had they stood tall and made a demand. The first two were over simple things, each to do with the war in the gulf. Each Bush owed him a favour, and one day, he would collect.

"What do you want with the islands?" Johan asked, suspicious as well as keen to add to his knowledge base for future reference.

"Come on, Johan, you know me better than that." The director smiled. "Besides, it is better you do not know."

"Agreed. So, where are you taking me?" Johan downed his drink and moved to pour himself another.

"We are heading to the US. We will land in Washington, and provided we get all of the negotiations out of the way by then, a plane will be ready to take you back home." Being the director of the NSA, Sikke Werkhoven had access to anything he wanted or needed. His courteous nature knew no bounds whenever he was in control.

"Well, I have the islands, and you want them. I do not. It seems to me that the only thing we need to agree on is the price. I cannot see that taking us longer than the flight." Johan smiled and raised his glass in salute.

By the time the plan landed several hours later, the two men had moved through the business negotiations, ensured that the payment had been made, processed, and the paper trail destroyed. For all his wealth, it never failed to amaze Johan just what could be done with modern technology, even from thirty thousand feet above the Atlantic Ocean.

As promised, there was a plane waiting for Johan the minute they stepped onto the tarmac in DC. He shook hands with Director Werkhoven. "Pleasure doing business with you," he said with a smile and a slight bow of his head.

Johan settled into the aircraft and waited as a groggy and restrained Godfrey was led aboard.

"Unlock him whenever you like, but wait until we are gone," one of the guards said, throwing a set of handcuff keys at Johan.

The men made a quick exit, the doors closed and the plane moved into position in a matter of minutes. The young stewardess had seen worse, and knew better than to ask what was going on. She smiled sweetly and unlocked the handcuffs with the keys Johan handed her.

"He will take it better if you do it, trust me." Johan smiled, noting how the stewardess was of Asian origins.

They clearly remembered the previous two instances where Godfrey had come to and knocked out three of the secret service agents that had been carrying him to his seat.

"Enjoy your flight. If I can get you anything, don't be afraid to ask," she said, smiling as she walked back towards the cockpit.

They took off and Johan settled into his chair. A rich man before the day started, the price he agreed with the US government was twice as much as he had expected to get. He had learned early in his life that the Americans would pay more for shit that other people would want for half the price.

"They did it again, didn't they," Godfrey grumbled, rubbing his neck.

"Yes, yes they did." Johan nodded and smiled. "Don't worry, Godfrey, they made it more than worth our while."

CHAPTER 10

The early morning sun streamed through the windows. Dr. Nattie Rose got out of bed and padded across the room to the window. The air conditioning was cool on her skin. Her nipples hardened as she walked.

Stretching, she stared out over the island at the thick expanse of green trees, the volcano rising up from their midst, and the sparkling blue of the ocean all around her. She was at peace for the first time in many years.

Turning, she saw the bed was empty. Her partner from the night before was long gone, his pillow cold since the pre-dawn hours.

She didn't care. The night before had been amazing, and she knew the work schedule that the guards had to keep.

Nick was worked like a slave. She hated his job, almost as much as he did.

It pays the bills, he would say whenever the subject came up in conversation. *Besides, it means I get to stay here with you.* He always ended with that line, and Nattie fell for it every time. She had to, because she feared she was falling in love with the young security guard. That concept terrified her. Her heart could not take being broken again. The cracks were so deep it barely held together as it was.

Showered and dressed, Nattie made herself a coffee and headed down to the main lab. The place was busy, as everybody came down and started making small talk.

Dr. Ian Matthews stood comparing notes and readings with his assistant Remi Henry. The small French-African man's head was nodding furiously as he scrambled to note down everything being said.

On the far side of the lab, Drs. Jones and Hepburn were stood side by side, bent over a table, no doubt studying the readouts from the nightly data analysis run. The two women were near inseparable. Having not known each other before the work on the island began, they got on like a house on fire.

Nattie thought they were a couple, but knew better than to ask. The women had it tough at times, with the sexually charged men of Black Arrow security always ready with a cat call or an invitation to their lodgings.

Rob Reddan was waiting at Nattie's desk, a coffee in hand ready for his boss. Seeing the cup, Nattie drained the one she was holding, and swapped it out for the full cup.

"How are things looking here?" she asked, picking up the top file and scanning her way through the data.

"Subject seventeen had a good night. The vitals are stabilizing and the wounds are healing nicely. There is no sign of infection or anything like that," Rob replied, perky and chirpy as always.

"That's good, but what are you hiding?" Nattie asked, pounding on the small tell that she had learned to spot in her assistant's demeanour.

"I was getting to that. We lost numbers seven, nine, and fourteen last night," he answered, looking at the floor as he spoke.

"How the heck did we lose fourteen? She was one of the strongest," Nattie said, shocked.

Rob looked at the floor, wilting under the curious gaze of his boss. "Um, well, you see there was a problem with the cages. Number twelve managed to get through the bars and well ... it wasn't pretty."

For a moment, Nattie did not know what to say. She remained silent gathering her thoughts. "But number twelve was a third of the size, and docile," she said, reiterating her surprise.

"Yes, ma'am, but this attack seemed ... um ... it seems to have been sexually motivated." Rob blushed as he mentioned such activities to his boss. At twenty-one years of age, Rob was no virgin, college had seen to that, but he had never met anybody as beautiful and openly sexual as Dr. Nattie Rose.

"Wow, well, I guess that means we should discontinue trials on that strain also." Nattie bit her bottom lip, chewing on the inside as she thought. "At least we have narrowed down our options even further. Now let me hear the good news."

They walked through the lab, stopping off at each of the six main stations. Early morning protocol dictated that every scientist be available to give an update on both their main stations and the linked sub-stations. The worst part of the job as far as Nattie was concerned were the volumes of paperwork she needed to complete each day. Not only did they rob her of hours of sleep, but only served to worsen her caffeine addiction.

The other stations had not experienced any significant losses or reading changes overnight. There were some fluctuations, but everything appeared to be normalizing. Stability was increasing. They had not had an explosion in almost two weeks.

After informing her team about the sudden sexual aggression in subjects treated with strain twelve, the decision was made to have them destroyed. The risk was great, and while the side effect could have interesting potential, it was not part of their core mission.

They gathered up the test subjects, secured them in a transport container, and waited for security to come and dispose of them. It would be more paperwork, but certainly for the best.

"Okay, people, let's get back to it. This island is not going to advance itself," Nattie stated, offering her customary, but not daily instruction to the team.

Everybody responded well to Nattie. The team in the central building all reported to her, which meant her morning routine was repeated on the second level lab. The Culture Shop, as the residents christened it, was where the treatment strains were created; microbiology at its finest.

Two teams of seven manned the stations, with an additional staff of interns and junior-level employees, each one thoroughly vetted and investigated by the US government before being given the position.

The requirement to leave their families behind meant that almost all of the employees, at least those under Nattie's command, were single. One, Dr. Malcom Prentiss was divorced, but the separation was far from pleasant.

Recognized as being one of the best in her field, Nattie had been hired as the lead scientist, and from day one, had bene accepted by the group. Professionals, all equally dedicated to the cause, their passion was their work, and were happy to let somebody else deal with the paperwork and logistics of things. Motivated by discovery rather than money, the team fit together well.

It took several weeks for the awkwardness and close quarters to feel less rigid and more like a home, but since then, they had developed a familial bond. They chatted, they laughed, and they worked. Everything had a time and a place. There had been no major arguments or quarrels. The transition had gone smoother than Nattie could have hoped for, and as a result, their findings and the results of the research were being reached ahead of schedule.

They had endured several failures along the way, especially in the first few weeks, but once the spectacle of the islands' native species wore off, and their knowledge of dosage strengths improved, then everything began to settle.

Nattie sat in her office, working her way through the morning reports as she prepared her own, which would be passed back to the mainland. With everything looking so promising, she had no doubt that their continued successes would bring positive feedback from her employers.

The task assigned to the group was simple. They were to use the local wildlife as test subjects for a range of biological and biochemical agents. It was mad-science, the kind of thing frowned upon by many, but the sort of work that appealed to the creative mind. For the people in the field of molecular biology, especially within the military branches connected to warfare and counter-terrorism, there was nothing more exciting.

With three remaining strands of the second run of strains still thriving, this round of testing looked promising. There was a buzz growing amongst the group, a belief that they were on the verge of their first major breakthrough. It brought with it a lift and a brightening of spirits, which only served to increase productivity and excitement for their product even more.

A knock at the door startled her. "Come in," she called.

Rob Reddan appeared, his closely cropped head of hair peering round the doorway. As young as he was, he had a naive nervousness about him that Nattie found charming. She liked the kid and had plans to build up his role as they went along.

"Sorry, but the security guy's here. To get rid of the twelves," he spoke.

"What, oh, right, sorry, I forgot. Do you think you could take them?" Nattie asked, looking at the pile of papers that still needed her attention.

"Um … I can do, I guess," Rob stuttered. "It's just, they are still alive."

Nattie stopped writing and looked up at her young assistant. "Okay, I'll do it this time," she said, getting up from her desk with a sigh. "But you need to countersign all of those requisition forms for me."

Rob nodded and moved behind the desk. He had a brilliant mind and did not mind the paperwork, but his soft heart never failed to surprise her. A clinical and precise man when it came to the experiments, he could not stand to be part of putting creatures to sleep.

The security guard had already loaded the container onto the trolley jack, well versed in the workings of the lab.

"Morning, Ferry," Nattie said as she walked out of her office and up to the guard.

"Hey, Dr. Rose," Ferry answered.

Ferry was an old hand at working Black Arrow Security. He had worked for them his entire career. A beast of a man, he had been all set for a glorious football career, until an unlucky tackle shattered his knee and sent all chances of a sporting career down the drain. Even now, fifteen years later, he still weighed in at over three hundred pounds, but was fitter that many of the men he worked with. His skin was a dark caramel colour, and his smile never failed to light up a room. No matter what day, what time, Ferry was always smiling.

"Shame we have to keep meeting like this," he said, the smile tempered but refused to be wiped from his face. He patted the large container. "Shall we?"

"After you, I insist," Nattie said, falling in behind him as they made their way down the hall.

A lift shaft had been installed to take people from the lab area to the incinerator. No other section of the building had such luxury. It was stairs all the way.

The incinerator room was at the end of a bare-brick corridor. No matter what the weather on the island, the corridor never rose above a chilly temperature. The burner, as people referred to it, was in its own room. Bare brick walls and a lingering metallic smell made the room Nattie's least favourite place on the island—

in the whole world for that matter—yet the nature of her job brought her down with alarming frequency.

"These ones are still alive," Ferry said, surprised.

"Yes, this time they are," Nattie answered, standing as close to the door as she could, without it being too obvious that she wanted to escape.

Ferry shrugged his shoulders and turned on the furnace. It burst into life with a whoosh of gas and a ball of flame. Working quickly, Ferry reached in, grabbed two cages and threw them into the fire. They had to weight a good twenty kilos each, but Ferry tossed them as if they were nothing.

"Ah, you bastard. Doc, watch out," Ferry cried out. A heavy clatter echoed around the room, and suddenly, three of the creatures were loose.

"Ferry, look out," Nattie cried. She saw the blood spurting from his hand, which she saw was missing two fingers.

"Get out of here, Doc," Ferry pleaded with her as he kicked out at one of the puppy-sized lizards.

The creature jumped into the air, evading the heavy boot swung its way. Landing on Ferry's thick leg, it scurried up his body, its claws drawing blood as it moved.

Ferry cried out and swatted at the creature. Grabbing it with his uninjured hand, he went to throw it, but the other two set on him. They sank their teeth into his flesh, and in a savage frenzy, tore his throat open. Ferry tried to scream, but all he managed to produce was a gargled rush of hot air.

Ferry fell to his knees, his eyes wide and staring. The creatures were ravenous, tearing further and further into his flesh until they chewed all the way through and his head fell away from his body. Hitting the floor with a dull thud, it rolled a ways before coming to rest.

Turning to run, Nattie saw one of the creatures had blocked her escape. It tilted its head as it rose onto its hind legs. The shorter front arms were raised, like a boxer ready for a fight.

It jumped, and Nattie moved to one side. The others made their move. One leaped onto her shoulders, mounting her from behind. Teeth sank into her flesh, and the warmth of free-flowing blood soon washed over her right-hand side. Thrashing around, Nattie managed to shake the creature loose. It fell to the floor, and the other moved to replace it.

There was a second door in the room and Nattie sprinted for it, ducking as she heard a hiss escape the closest of the number twelve strain creatures. The creature sailed over her head, snapping at her, only to collide with the metal door. Its head did not crack, but the flesh split and a thick blackish blood dribbled from the wound. Skin flaps peeled backwards from its skull, covering its eyes, which were positioned high on its skull.

Grabbing at the door, Nattie pulled. It didn't move. Remembering her key card, she fumbled in her pocket. Swiping the card, the door chirped and the lock opened.

Trying the door again, it came open with ease, and a rush of warm, tropical air washed over her. Nattie fell from the room, collapsing into the grass.

Before she could get back to her feet, the three creatures were outside. One jumped on her chest, pinning Nattie to the floor. The long claws of its feet digging into her chest, and more painfully, the bite mark on her shoulder. Crying out, hoping to gain the guards attention, she waited for the end to come.

The creature pinning her down leaned its head in close, nostrils flaring and closing, sniffing its prey.

Without warning, it stood up straight, its rear claws stabbing into Nattie's stomach as it sought for purchase to keep itself steady. Sniffing at the air, the creature bolted, closely followed by the second. The third of the surviving number twelve strain stumbled out of the building, half-collapsing into the grass. It disappeared into the trees, following its brothers, the flaps of unfurled skin wafting in their air like wings.

Nattie lay on the floor for a moment, lost to the undulating waves of pain that wracked her body. The stabbing pains in her chest from where the creature's claws had punctured her skin were nothing compared to the burning in her shoulder.

The ground was slick with her blood. It squelched as she rolled over and rose to her knees. Dizzy, both from the loss of blood as well as the receding flow of adrenaline, she made it to her feet. Stumbling, she walked around the building, leaning against the wall, her bloodied shoulder creating a crimson smear, like a blood-leaking snail.

"Help me," Nattie called out, her voice growing weak as her strength ebbed away.

She collapsed to the floor by the main gates. She heard the commotion as the guards caught sight of her. Hearing a familiar voice, she looked up and promptly collapsed to the floor. Darkness engulfed her, swallowing the world in a single bite.

CHAPTER 11

Nattie came too, and for a moment, she thought that she was flying. Her body floated above the floor, and the world passed by around her. She remembered the attack, and her escape from the incinerator. Her vision focused, and the three guards came into view. They carried her through the building. She recognized the ceiling of the main entrance hall.

"We need to get out there. Strain twelve ... three of them ... Ferry ... dead." Nattie forced the words out of her mouth, each uttered syllable made her dizzier and dizzier.

"What is she saying?" Rob Reddan called as he jogged down the corridor.

He had heard the commotion and been elected by the staff in the main lab to head out and investigate. He did not know about Nattie's injuries until he saw her, although the blood trail that led him to the group had him expecting trouble.

"She said we have a breach," a gruff sounding voice spoke up. "Some of those freaks you guys work with escaped."

Rob turned around and saw the grizzly face of Mark Hunter staring at him. His thick, square jaw was covered in a thick grey stubble, and his cold, steel-blue eyes bored into their target like lasers.

"She was ... she was down at the incinerator. We had an issue with one of the strains, and they needed to be destroyed. She went down with ... oh crap, what's his name ... the big guy, always smiling, Terry?" Rob racked his brain, trying to pull the specifics out of the panicked fog.

"Ferry?" one of the men carrying Nattie spoke.

"Yes, that's him. She went down to the incinerator with Ferry." Rob stopped walking and was flattened by Hunter, who either did not see, or more likely, did not care, that the scientist had come to a halt.

"What kind of issue?" Hunter growled. He leaned in close, an odour of tobacco breath and cheap aftershave wafted into Rob's face.

"Well, overnight one of the subjects injected with strain twelve of our—" Rob began.

"I don't give a shit about your science mumbo-jumbo. What happened? How big is it, and can we kill it? Real details, not wizardry crap," Hunter snapped, looking at the three men standing still, holding the bleeding doctor between them. "Get her to the infirmary, Jesus fucking wept."

The three men near ran from the hallway, eager to be out of range from Hunter's notorious bad attitude.

"One of the subjects got out of its cage. Kills another one. They showed increased levels of sexual aggression that were off the charts. We decided to terminate the entire strain. They are small, the size of a puppy. Quick, strong, but well, they are alive, so they can be killed." Rob swallowed, unsure if his answers were going to keep the gruff security chief happy.

"Goddammit, you science types grind my balls. Guess you expect us to clean up the mess downstairs too." Hunter stared at Rob, who felt his body turn to jelly.

"Um … the creatures … they have tracking devices," Rob stuttered.

"Tracking devices?"

"Yeah, when we bring them in, we chip them, mainly for identification, they all look alike, you know. Anyway, they can be used for tracking too, pretty accurate, down to a few feet," Rob spoke quicker and quicker. Excited at first, but soon merely desperate to get the words out.

"Get back to your lab and make sure no more accidents happen." Hunter shoved Rob out of the way and moved off down the hall. "Flewitt, Abbott, Lopez, front and centre. Looks like we are taking a walk."

Even after the man had disappeared, the lingering memory of his presence was an imposing object.

Rob turned and hurried back to the lab. He knew people would be anxious for an update.

***

The four men stood in silence, waiting for the outer gate to open. The central building's fortification had a single main exit point. A double-layered gate that ensured the compound was never exposed. The exit door from the incinerator room was an emergency exit door that only opened one way, held secure by a powerful electromagnet.

As they stood between the walls, the hum of the electrified fence was loud. The generators stood a matter of feet from them and created enough noise to rival a jet plane.

Slowly, the main doorway opened and the jungle beyond came into view. It was the first time that any of the Black Arrow group had stepped foot beyond the compound for anything more than to empty the traps.

The volcano towered up above them, its side covered with trees. The earth immediately beyond the compound was stripped bare and dead. Tree stumps sprouted from the ground at regular intervals, showing the progress of the construction team, but for the rest, the ground was barren.

The trees began suddenly, and with a density that rivalled any environment Mark Hunter had ever seen. His time in both the military and Black Arrow had taken him to some of the darkest parts of the globe, yet he had never seen a jungle quite like the one on the Black Arrow Archipelago.

"We stick together, move through the trees in a diamond formation. I'll take point. Flewitt, I want you on the left, Abbott on the right. Lopez, I want you and that cannon of yours to bring up the rear. We don't know what is waiting for us out there, so stay alert," Hunter said into the microphone mounted to his helmet.

"What are we looking for anyway?" Lopez asked. A short man with muscles atop his muscles, he was a powerhouse like no other in the unit. There was a running joke that his center of gravity was so low, he had never fallen over, not even as a child.

"I have no clue what those guys have been doing. Unit Two I can understand, but the micro shit those guys are working with? Chemicals and viruses and shit? Fuck no, that stuff should be left alone," Hunter snarled.

The group moved through the trees, their footsteps crunching on the foliage-covered ground. A path appeared, and they moved to follow it. After having moved no more than a few meters into the trees, the world changed.

It was as if they had moved through some sort of temporal rift and ended up in a different time and space. The jungle closed around them, and the compound disappeared from view.

The sounds of jungle life sprang up. The chirp of insects and the rustle of underbrush as things scurried about close to the ground. Each new noise put the men further on edge. They knew what lived in the trees. They had seen the small creatures being caught in the scientist's traps and had all hear the thunderous growls that came from deeper in the trees.

Hunter led the group, his steps never faltering in spite of the nerves that were firing inside his body. He was not lying when he voiced is distrust of the scientists' work being done in the main lab. The concept of playing with other creatures' genetic make-up, DNA and whatever else, terrified him. Humans were not gods and had no right to act like them.

He moved in a straight line through the trees, following the tracking device the scrawny-looking scientist had given him.

A few meters later, it gave a beep. They were close. Stopping the group, he pointed into the trees to his right. "Abbott, we've got one up ahead, ten feet or so. Keep your eyes peeled."

"Roger that, sir," Abbott replied.

"Remember, shoot to kill, and keep it was quiet as possible. We don't want to draw any unnecessary attention to ourselves," Hunter added as an afterthought.

"Yes, sir," Abbott replied, pulling the silenced pistol from its holster.

Each of the men had armed themselves with a pistol and a hunting knife. All but Lopez had chosen to carry and M16, while he chose an AA12. It was a favourite of his, and while the armoury only carried one, everybody knew to leave it for Lopez. There was even a hand-written sign with that very warning written on it posted above the weapon.

Abbott pushed away from the group, rounding a large tree. Beyond it, he saw a small clearing. He saw nothing, but at the same time had no idea what he was looking for. The only description they had was greenish-brown, and the size of a puppy. Not much to go on, especially in a jungle filled with monsters.

Something moved, scurrying on the periphery of his vision. Abbott spun around, but whatever he had seen, it was gone.

Turning again, he stopped. Sitting at the base of the tree, he saw what they had been sent to find.

The creature was crouched down on all fours, its short front legs clearly not designed or sustained use in such a fashion.

The creature had a tail almost as long as its body, and head that looked to end in a beak. It turned its head to stare at Abbott, studying him.

Abbott squeezed the trigger of his pistol and with a gentle whoosh, the creature's head exploded in a cloud of blood, brain, and skull fragments.

The creature's now headless body crumpled into the ground a pool of blood spreading around it.

Abbott moved through the trees and back to the group. He looked over his shoulder as he went, unable to shake the feeling that there was something else out there, watching him.

"One down," he said, reporting back to the group, who had moved on ahead in search of the other two escapees.

"We are up ahead, a few hundred meters. We have one in the trees, and another on the ground. Hold back, this won't take us long," Hunter replied, his voice hushed.

Abbott stopped where he was and looked around. The jungle was close, and hot. The air was misty and sweet tasting. Abbott stopped trying to wipe away the sweat from his face because the jungle offered no respite.

Something moved in the trees around him. Abbott turned and looked, but once again, saw nothing but jungle. The trees seemed to move. It was like being stuck in a house of mirrors at a carnival. The maze of mirrored walls. Everything looked the same. It was disorienting to the point where he had to close his eyes to stop the world from spinning.

When he opened them again, Abbott knew he was not alone. Moving only his eyes, he looked to his left. He saw the creature through the trees, the way people say ghosts can be seen only when on the periphery of human vision.

A sharp, orange-coloured eye watched Abbott, staring him down.

"Abbott, we got one, but the other is coming back your way." Hunter's voice rang in his ears.

Abbott caught his breath, flinching as he watched the creature watching him.

"Abbott, Jesus fuck, man, answer me. The third target is heading your way. Do you copy?" Hunter's voice boomed. The man's normally thin patience non-existent beyond the compound walls.

Abbott moved his hand and pressed the button to open the comms link. "I can't talk. Hold your position," he whispered, trying to talk without moving his lips.

The momentary distraction offered by the communication resulted in his focus falling away from the creature in the trees. Searching, Abbott tried to find sight of it again, but all he saw were trees.

Turning, slowly, he looked further, but the creature was gone. In spite of the heat, Abbott realized he was no longer covered in sweat.

He knew the creature was still close by. He could feel its presence.

"Abbott, come in, we lost you there, buddy," Flewitt's voice came back over the comms. "We are heading your way. Hold tight, buddy." Paul Flewitt had known Chris Abbott for many years, yet this was only the second time they had actually worked together on a job.

Abbott wanted to answer, to tell them once again to hold their ground, but before he could open the communication again, they appeared.

Hunter stormed through the trees, his stride filled with purpose. His eyes targeted the frozen Abbott, but even the heat of their angry glare could not melt the terror from his limbs.

Behind Hunter, Flewitt and Lopez emerged, moving slower, with more caution than their leader.

"When I give you an order, you answer me, goddammit," Hunter roared.

Abbott wanted to reply, but there was no point. Hunter could not hear him, because his head had been swallowed by the raptor-like dinosaur that had ripped it from his body.

The creature swallowed the head in one bite, gulping at it like a feeding crocodile, while a shower of blood slicked its belly.

Hunter's body remained standing, only falling when the raptor nudged it.

A burst of gunfire from Flewitt's M16 shattered the relative silence of the jungle. The rounds tore a fist-sized hole into the creature's flank, punching through its body to create a tear the other side also.

The raptor turned, raising its head to let out a battle cry. The head exploded with a whoosh as the frag grenade launched from Lopez's AA12 landed in its mouth. The body was blown backwards into the trees, colliding with the nearest trunk with enough force to snap the creature's spine.

The echo of the explosion rang in Abbott's ears, while a sticky layer of pulverised dino flesh covered his front.

"We need to move, now." Flewitt took charge, grabbing his friend by the shoulders, shaking him until Abbott showed signs of response. "Chris, move, we need to hightail it back to the compound."

No sooner had Flewitt spoke than two more raptors appeared behind them. Lopez spun, opening fire on the two, his 12-gauge unloading a burst of ten rounds in two seconds. Lopez died with his finger on the trigger, dealing a bloody death to one of the creatures as a fourth tore open his stomach, greedily swallowing the steaming organs that spewed from the gash in his belly.

The second of the two approaching creatures had taken two rounds to the flank and had been put to the floor, where it lay gasping. Its legs kicked at the air, like a dog caught in a dream, before it fell still.

The fourth raptor, distracted by the bounty took a double burst of hot lead, spewed simultaneously from Flewitt and Abbott's M16's.

The creature managed to turn and advance on them before it stumbled under the weight of its own frame. It crashed into the mud, and was still alive as the two men ran for the compound.

The sound of their altercation with the raptors brought the jungle to life.

The ground seemed to rumble, and somewhere behind them, a roar made the trees shudder to the roots.

"I think we woke something up," Abbott said as they burst through the trees, the compound just ahead of them.

"Shut up and run," Flewitt panted. Not as fit as he used to be, the skirmish and run left him empty. He stumbled in the grass.

Falling to one knee, he thrust his hands out to push his body back to a vertical base. His rifle slid forward and over his head in the process. Turning, caught in half a mind to grab the weapon, Flewitt caught sight of the creature just too late.

It landed on him with a jump and sent him falling to the ground. The creature was a shade over hip height dug and scratched at Flewitt's chest. The razor-sharp claws tore through the material of his uniform and bulletproof vest, down to the skin, and then deeper still.

Strands of flayed flesh and lumps of scooped-out meat were thrown aside as the creature continued to burrow into the man's cheek. Ribs cracked and splintered, emerging around the edges of the spreading wound like the hungry edges or the Sarlacc pit.

Fumbling, Flewitt managed to move his pistol and fire a burst of four shots into the creature's belly.

The skin tore open and long, looping strands of intestines fell, covering Flewitt with their slimy gore. The stench that came from within the creature was intense. It gave a cry and fell backwards, landing on the bare ground.

"Help me," Flewitt called to his friend, blood bubbling from his mouth in a froth.

"Come on, buddy," Abbott cried, rooting for his friend to crawl away while he remained rooted to the spot.

More of the small creatures appeared, at least half a dozen in total, from the shapes Abbott could make out.

Flewitt clawed at the ground, dragging his mutilated body closer to the compound. He knew he was a dead man, but he would not go down without a fight.

"Run," he called to his friend.

Abbott turned and fled towards the compound gates.

Flewitt raised his pistol and tried to focus his blurring vision. He saw the shapes of the creatures closing in on him. He closed one eye, said a silent prayer to whichever deity was listening, and pulled the trigger until the weapon clicked empty.

He tried not scream as the creatures pulled him apart, but it was a step too far. His cries were cut off when the hungry beasts reached his throat, but by then, Abbott and the men guarding the gate, had all heard enough.

"Close it, close it," Abbott cried as he doubled over and vomited.

"The others?" a voice called out.

"Dead," Abbott replied between heaves.

From above them, in the watch tower, gunfire rang out; a heavy burst of automatic fire. A blanket strike, no finesse or precision. They were sweeping for anything that happened to be in the line of fire.

It seemed to take an age before the rattle of gunfire stopped. When it did, the silence was just as terrifying.

Abbott hauled himself to his feet, and turned to look at the soldiers around him.

"Back to your stations. We need double guards on the towers, and pump full power into the grid. I want that wall buzzing." With Hunter and Lopez dead, command of the main compound fell to Abbott, a position he did not consider himself ready to assume.

"Yes, sir," the voices answered, and everybody got back to their duties.

Abbott took himself to the lab. He was tired. He needed coffee, and cigarettes in lethal quantities, but more than both, he needed answers. He needed to understand what those things were, the creatures that escaped. One of them was still out there, and while he did not particularly want to go back outside the compound, they could ill-afford to have a genetically altered beast running amok.

His stomach flipped and flopped at the thought of the call he needed to make back to the offices in Washington. They were pushing hard for results. Hunter had been involved in daily check-ins and meetings with the senior scientists that controlled and confirmed results over the net. Now, with Hunter's headless body decomposing beyond the compound walls, Abbott would be thrown to the lions.

Abbott stopped in the hallway. His mind yanked away to thoughts of Hunter's body. Would it still be in the forest? Would the creatures have come back and eaten the rest of him? What about something else? Abbott pinched himself, trying to break up the images of his overactive imagination. When that didn't work, he raised a hand and slapped himself across the face. His cheek burned, but the image of Hunter's shredded corpse dissolved, and the inner sanctum of the compound came into focus.

The main lab lay to his right. The door was sealed and the windows blanked out. He knew they would be in there. The outbreak would be just as nerve-wracking for them as for the security detail.

Abbott took a deep breath and knocked on the lab door.

CHAPTER 12

Nattie woke up in the sick bay. An IV tube extended from her left arm. Her head ached like a bad hangover. She tried to move, and everything started to ache.

Lying back down, Nattie closed her eyes. Fog clouded her head, but she remembered everything that had happened. Turning her head, she looked at her right shoulder. A large white bandage covered her upper body. Thicker over her injuries, it extended tight across her chest and under her left arm. Old blood stained the white bandage a rust colour.

Nattie wiggled her fingers, breathing a sigh of relief when each one moved when she tried it.

"Ah, you are awake," a voice spoke after a long, timeless period of solitude. In movies, the doctor or nurse always happened to walk in just as the patient was waking up. No such luck on the island.

"Hey," Nattie smiled, looking to find Nick standing in the doorway.

Dressed in his uniform, he smiled when Nattie looked at him.

"I was worried about you," he said, walking up to the bed. Leaning down, kissing Nattie on her cheek, he paused in position for a moment, and then, when her head turned towards him, on the lips.

"I'm tougher than I look. Those things, Strain Twelve, they escaped. They killed Ferry." Nattie flinched, sitting upright in bed.

"Hey, hey, easy there." Nick placed his hands on her shoulders and gently laid her back in the bed. "It's all been taken care of."

"Already," Nattie asked, shocked and a little confused.

"Yes, we sent a group out after them." Nick paused.

"What is it?" Nattie asked, sitting up in bed once more, a cold ball forming in her gut.

"We um … we lost some guys." Nick lowered his eyes to the floor.

"Who?" Nattie asked. She did not know many of the security team, but Nick did, and it was important for her to be there for him.

"Hunter, Flewitt, and Lopez." Nick raised his gaze. His eyes were red from holding back the tears. "Flewitt was a good guy."

"I'm sorry. What … was it the Strain Twelve subjects?" Nattie cringed at the sound of the question. She asked for purely selfish reasons, and that hurt her also.

"What? Oh, no, no, it was something else. Abbott survived, he is in charge now. Although, nobody has seen him in a couple of days. He has been locked away—"

"Days?" Nattie interrupted.

"Yes," Nick answered, his face showing his confusion. "Oh crap, you just woke up. Sorry, it was three days ago. You have been out ever since they brought you up here."

"No wonder I feel so stiff." Nattie moved to sit up again, waiting for Nick to stop her.

He did not.

"It could also be the injuries." As cute and as funny as he was, Nattie could not help but laugh at how dense he could be from time to time.

"It's a good thing you are pretty," she said with a laugh. "Help me get out of bed. I need to check in at the lab."

Nick stood and moved to the bed. He did not stop Nattie, but also make no direct attempt to help her.

"I don't think that is a good idea," he began.

"I need to get to the lab. I've rested enough. It's just my arm that got hurt, and I don't need that to walk and talk." Nattie stared at Nick, her eyes set, her jaw clenched.

"Dr. Hendricks said you should stay on bed rest. They have you on antibiotics, because of the bite wounds," Nick began, but before he could finish, Nattie grabbed him and pulled herself to her feet. "I need a shirt."

Nick convinced Nattie to wait for him to get her some clean clothes. On his way out, he spoke to Dr. Hendricks, who did not seem surprised or against Nattie getting up and about.

Moving gingerly, her body still disagreeing with her decision to get out of bed, Nattie moved through the main building in the direction of her lab. Nick had stayed with her for a while, but had to leave for his shift to start. He promised to check in on her later. Nattie knew that meant he would be along to make sure she was taking it easy and not overdoing it.

The lab was in full swing. Nattie stood in the cleaning room watching through the window. Lathering layer after layer on her hands, she smiled. Rob moved through the stations, watching and checking, answering questions offering advice where needed. She knew he had what it took to step up when needed. He just needed to be pushed into the deep-end of the pool.

Rinsing her hands, and sliding her arms into her lab coat, Nattie entered the lab. Her shoulder hurt, the act of getting dressed and now donning her lab attire pained her more than she would care to admit.

The doors opened and everything stopped. Faces turned to look in her direction and all sounds ceased to exist. She felt like a stranger walking in a Wild West saloon.

A wave of relief swept through the room, moving like a wave, travelling from person to person until it reach Rob, who stood with tears in his eyes

Nattie walked into the room and Rob swept her into a hug. "We were worried about you," he said.

The embrace made Nattie's should sing in agony, but she bit her lip as best she could.

"So, what's been going on here?" she asked.

"Let's grab a coffee and I will fill you in," Rob suggested.

"That is the best idea I have ever heard." Nattie smiled and followed Rob through to her office.

CHAPTER 13

"Hugo, this is Abbott, do you read?" Abbott sat in the main security office on the upper level of the core compound.

He took long, deep drags on his cigarette while waiting for an answer. It was eleven thirty at night, and outside a storm was raging unlike anything he had ever seen.

The rain fell in sheets, pouring so heavy it looked like a bucket being emptied just above the window.

"Abbott, I read you. This storm is a bitch, and the weather stations say it is only just getting started," Hugo Estevez answered.

"Just wanted to check in. This thing is really raging down here. I'm pulling the guys from the towers for the night. This storm is only getting worse and it is not worth it." Abbott crushed the cigarette and immediately lit another.

"Already one step ahead of you. We are doubling down here. Going to ride this baby out with a smile and some scotch we scored from the last supply chopper," Hugo answered.

"Alright, hang tight, brother," Abbott said, leaning back in his chair to watch the storm through the window.

Storms fascinated Christopher Abbott. Ever since he was a child, he would watch them roll in, counting the time between the lightning and thunder. He had seen his fair share of tornadoes and summer storms over the years, but even he could not ignore the way his skin seemed to tingle as the storm drew closer.

Darkness had settled over the island a lot earlier than normal. The clouds started gathering in the mid-morning, holding their distance while their forces grew.

The wind came first. It was a cold, biting wind that blew away the heat of the island, replacing it with a wintry surge that drove everybody that did not need to be there indoors.

From inside the lab, Nattie and her team worked with the gentle tunes of the lab's music system, providing them a gentle soundtrack that helped them all through their day. Their lab had no windows, no direct view of the outside world, rendering them oblivious to the raging weather and rough seas.

As the afternoon wore on, the rain began. They were fat drops at first, which pelted the ground like artillery fire. This soon increased to a downpour. Abbott was sure the technical term would be monsoon for how much rain fell. By mid-afternoon, even that word was redundant. He had never seen rain like it in all his years.

The storm itself set in early evening, Mother Nature moving all of her pieces into place, throwing an assault at them which exceeded their darkest nightmares.

The windows in the security office rattled and shook in their frames. Three of the spotlights that surrounded the perimeter blew in a billowing fountain of sparks and flame. A direct strike from the storm saw to it that the northern corner of the compound was cast into darkness.

One by one, Abbott recalled his men, bringing them inside to safety. They were not taken off watch. In fact, he doubled the watch for the night, just in case.

After twelve hours of battering, the storm only appeared to be growing stronger. Something in it worried Abbott; the kind of worry that starts deep in the gut, planting its roots and finding a sturdy home there before spreading. Try as he might, Abbott could not shake a feeling of urgency and growing finality that surrounded every whip of lightning, and each rumbling wave of thunder.

The lashing rain reduced the effectiveness of the remaining lights to next to nothing. Their high-powered beams were barely able the combat the elements and reach the ground.

There was something else in it too. Abbott was sure of that. He began scanning the darkness, making sense and shapes out of the black. His eyes picked spots that seemed blacker, somehow. Malignant shadows, with evil intentions.

Not a man to spook easily, Abbott shuddered as he lit another cigarette. The ashtray was full, overflowing even, and so he had taken to using the leftover coffee cup.

Lightning struck the nearest tower. The windows lit up amid the shower of sparks like disgruntled neighbours in a street of caterwauling drunks. The flare chased away the demons of Abbott's mind, forcing the darkness back a step.

The rate at which the thunder rumbled became almost constant, with only the smallest break coming between. It was a small chance to breathe, before the next suffocating wave of storm run though. On the edges of the islands, the sea was a furious body of water that lambasted the coastline with a violent assault that saw two different docks torn apart with ease. The chunks of wood torn free by the waves were either plucked and dragged out to sea or picked up by a spinning gust of stormy air, and flung back into the mainland.

Abbott moved down from the upper levels, moving to the ground floor. The impact of the storm on the building was less there. Had he not have been sitting upstairs for so long, lost to the battering of the storm, he would not have understood the severity of it at all. The rumbles echoed through the corridors, and the flashes lit up the darker corners of the building like a strobe light. Abbott felt his apprehension lessen by the minute.

***

The glass shattered, shards flew in all directions. The scream that followed rang out in the sealed lab, and made everybody turn and look.

"What happened?" Nattie called, scrambling from her office, her eyes wide.

"Nothing, Caroline dropped a vial. Non-toxic. No need for panic, people," Rob Reddan said, bending down to help clean up the pieces of glass.

"You don't need to help me," Caroline whispered.

Quiet, shy, and petite, Caroline had held Rob's eyes since the first day of operations. It was the kind of admiration that everybody else could see apart from the two people starring in the show.

"I don't mind," Rob answered, smiling.

Caroline blushed, her cheeks growing redder and redder until she needed to look away. Her long, dark brown hair fell over her face, covering her flushed cheeks.

"Thank you. Ouch," Caroline gasped, clutching at her thumb.

"Are you okay? What's wrong?" Rob asked, concerned.

"Nothing, I just cut my thumb on a piece of glass," Caroline said, trying to play down the injury.

The blood that dripped from her hand and onto the floor gave away the true extent of the wound, however. The deep red fluid stood out on the white, tiled floor of the lab.

"You need to get that seen to. Come on, let's clean it up and get you to the medical bay." Rob stood up and took charge. The change in his personality since Nattie's injury continued to manifest in all the right ways.

With Caroline's hand cleaned and bandaged, Rob took her out of the lab and to the medics, white Nattie cleaned up the rest of the glass.

"Did you know it was storming?" Caroline asked as the pair made their way down the corridor.

"I had no idea. I knew it could storm here, but this seems like a good one," Rob answered.

A gust of wind rattled the windows and the lighting flickered. Caroline gave a small scream and pressed herself tighter to Rob.

"I hate thunderstorms," she said, looking up at Rob.

"Well, we are safe in here. This building a fortress." Rob smiled.

The words fell from his mouth just as a window behind them blew inwards. The glass shattered, spinning out in all directions, thrown on a wild wind that charged through the gaping hole in the building's flank. The rush of air created a piercing howl that chased the pair down the corridor like a pack of wolves. Rain poured through, splattering on the linoleum flooring. Thunder rumbled and lightning cracked in simultaneous symphony. The sound was like a jet taking off mere feet from where they stood. It was deafening and powerful to the point of being a physical presence that both grabbed and shook them.

Caroline screamed, and in that moment, it felt as if they were lost. They were stranded in some crazy and violent land. The storm was their oppressor, chasing them down, intent on dealing out a punishment befitting their intrusion. The secure compound and the armed guards were thrown away. The knowledge that the rest of the team were working away oblivious to the storm, as they too had been until a few moments prior, ceased to exist in their consciousness.

Rob felt fear, absorbing it from Caroline, while at the same time it grew within him of its own accord.

The sudden change in the environment, the unexpected weather and the shattering window; too much, too fast. It seemed unnatural and out of place. In those few moments, his rational brain abandoned him, and he gave in to the child-like feeling of terror and helplessness.

It was only when a small break came in the storm, and the initial shock of the noise outside began to subside that things returned to a more acceptable level of normalcy.

"Let's keep moving. Nothing to do here. It's up to the Black Arrow guys to tidy up the mess," Rob said, his voice raised in order not to be drowned out by the howling din created beyond the walls.

Two corridors later, and the sounds of the storms receded back to the distant howl, the safe and secure howl that can only come from the danger being tucked away.

"Thank you for coming with me," Caroline said as they sat waiting for Dr. Hendricks to come back from his lunch.

"My pleasure. I mean, this place is safe and secure, but I don't like the idea of you walking around on your own." Rob's face started to deepen in shade as he spoke.

"I don't think the creatures beyond the walls would get to us," Caroline said, smiling.

"It's not them I am worried about. It's those Black Arrow guys. I don't like the idea of you being alone with some of them walking around," Rob stuttered as he spoke, but his newfound confidence held his voice. "I like you, Caroline."

"Oh … I, I like you too." Both blushed but held each other's gaze.

It was then that the power went out.

CHAPTER 14

Abbott finished making himself a fresh cup of coffee. The thick brown liquid smelled amazing as it was extracted from the tiny pods. Even the machine itself was a thing of beauty. Abbott had never seen eye-to-eye with his former boss, except, he recently learned, when it came to coffee.

The rich, brown drink was, in Abbott's own mind, a gift from the heavens. If anybody asked for divine proof, his answer would always be coffee. This was partly because he enjoyed the drink so much, and regarded it so highly, and partly because he held a strong dislike for organized religion, and any chance to rile some feathers with a snarky answer made him smile.

Sitting back down behind the desk, he sighed. Just as he took his cup from the machine, the storm knocked out the main power. There were back-up generators which would kick in, but they needed to be manually redirected from the third island so as not to waste energy on non-essential areas.

Abbott liked the silence, the sense of detachment. Ever since the deaths of Hunter and the others, Black Arrow had been sticklers for updates and work logs. Now, he was free of that for the moment. He had no chain of command to follow; the world was his.

Abbott took a sip of the coffee, the smooth taste of the double-strength espresso made his taste buds explode.

The emergency lights went out, plunging him into a sudden and total darkness. The rage of the storm outside increased to full pitch as every other background noise fell away.

Abbott made to rise from the chair, but in the darkness misplaced his coffee cup. The scolding hot liquid covered his leg, and while he cursed the darkness, he also thanked the coffee deity that he had not chosen a larger drink.

Flashlight in hand, he left the central office and headed out into the halls.

The storm buffeted the building, and somewhere, he heard people screaming.

A few moments later, a thunderous crash echoed through the building. The sound of the storm increased even more, and in the darkness, the building came alive.

Shouts and screamed echoed around him, bouncing off the walls in every direction. Pandemonium ensued with a dizzying impact. Abbott stood stunned, surrounded by noise, unsure which way to turn. The urgent cries and shrieks were coming from his own men.

The rattle of gunfire thawed him, forcing a surging wave of adrenaline through his body. Running, Abbott moved towards the main reception area.

In his head, he ran through the protocol, the only problem being, in all of the drills and training, Abbott had been a participant rather than the commanding officer.

More gunfire erupted; a short burst that ended in a sudden silence, like the calm before the worst of the storm. Christopher Abbott felt his blood freeze.

The silence only lasted a moment, not even a period of time that could be measured without use of some item of equipment, yet in it, he heard something. As the knowledge formed in his brain, the unthinkable had happened.

There was no time for him to finish the thought. He rounded the corner, moving at a run when his feet slid out from under him. His feed slapped at the floor as they tried to find purchase, but it was too late. He landed hard, his legs straight out before him. The impact was hard and jarring. Something popped in his back, but Abbott ignored it.

The floor was wet, and by the glow of his flashlight, Abbott could make out the viscous black-looking substance that caused the problem.

That's blood.

The notion dawned on him just as the smell hit, the sweet, metallic odour of slaughter.

Jumping to his feet, Abbott grabbed his torch and went for his gun. He only had his pistol with him, but anything was better than nothing.

Raising both light and weapon, he moved forward, slower now. Sweeping the light from floor to ceiling, his eyes scanning everything from far to near, he walked on.

The head that stared up at him was unrecognizable. The skin had been torn away and the bone was crushed like an empty can. Abbott caught the gag in his throat, but could not stop the tremor in his hands.

Images of what had happened before, of the creatures that lay beyond the compound walls played over and over in his head; a constant loop of the nightmare he had survived.

He had seen enough horror movies to know the survivors very rarely made it through the sequel.

Behind him, something moved in the darkness. The squelching sound of footsteps in blood spun Abbott around, his trigger fingers squeezing in reflex.

"Don't shoot, don't shoot," Rob cried out, throwing his hands up in the air while simultaneously moving before Caroline, who froze in the blinding glare of the flashlight.

"Jesus, you almost got yourself killed," Christopher said, lowering his gun quickly so that they did not see his trembling hands.

"What's going on?" Rob asked.

"Who are you?" Christopher did not recognize either of the two. He thought the man looked familiar, but he did not want to be too careful. The chance the terrorists or some black ops outfit had made a play for the island was slim, but no more so than a stampede of the indigenous wildlife.

"I'm Rob, and this is Caroline." Rob moved aside to Christopher take a good look at Caroline. "We are scientists. We were on our way to the medical bay, and holy shit, that's a head," Rob choked on his words as he caught the flashlight's beam reflecting in the decapitated cranium's eyes.

"Stick with me. I don't know what is going on," Abbott told them, looking from one to the other, "but having you here is safer than leaving you alone somewhere else."

"Have you tried the radio?" Rob asked, pointing to the old school walkie-talkie-style radio attached to Christopher's hip.

"Radio, no … actually, I didn't," Christopher stuttered, mad at himself.

"This is Abbott; I need an update. What's going on guys?" He waited, but got nothing but static back in response.

"That's not good," Caroline said. Her hands were clenched on Rob's shoulders.

"Cardos, Peacock, do you read?" Abbott raised his voice, near yelling into the radio.

"Abbott, we've been breached. The storm took out of the power. The fence went down and they attacked," a whispered voice answered.

The words spoken in such hushed tones that Abbott could not work out who answered him.

"Shouldn't the emergency power be on by now?" Caroline asked.

"Hold tight, we are coming to you. Give us a location." Abbott carried on as if he had not heard Caroline's question.

"We are in the mess hall, but stay away. There are three of them in here, and … and … they've seen me. Run, run!" The whisper turned into a scream. A rattle of gunfire sounded from the radio as well as exploding around them in real-time surround sound.

Caroline screamed again.

"Come on. Stick close to me. We need to get you guys somewhere safe while we seal this place off." Abbott took off into the darkness, stepping over the headless corpse lying a few feet further along.

Caroline followed, holding onto Rob as if he were a life preserver and she was drowning on a wild ocean.

They moved through the dark, taking the first left that came their way. The double doors to the canteen lay before them. The blood-smeared windows did not bode well for a simple procedure.

"You're not going in there, are you?" Caroline asked.

"My men are in there," Abbott answered, forcing the emotion from his voice. His leadership came with responsibilities, and he would not shirk on them.

"I can't," Caroline whimpered, but the doors burst open, and a large bipedal lizard the size of a man appeared. Its body was covered in blood, pooling beneath it as he stood. A long trail of intestines dangled from a hole in its flank, yet its eyes were still sharp. The yellow orbs seemed to glow in its head as it studied its prey.

Christopher raised his pistol, took careful aim, and fired. His body surged with adrenaline as his eyes focused on the creature standing before him.

One carefully placed round saw the creature's right eye explode with a surge of draining fluid and torn flaps of skin and eyeball. The beast gave a roar, faltered, and fell, collapsing in a heap that blocked the doorway.

Christopher worked his way over and around the mass of bleeding meat and disappeared into the canteen.

"I can't …" Caroline began to weep.

"Yes, you can. We have to," Rob told her, taking her hands into his. Even in the darkness, he could see the sparkle in her eyes.

"But …" she whispered, unsure what else to say.

"Just hold onto me," Rob said, as he too started to scale the carcass.

It was dark in the kitchen, but the backup generators powered up just as Caroline made it over her first obstacle.

The light was dim, the power needing to be spread over the entire compound. It was not dim enough, however, to hide the horrors that covered the canteen.

The walls and floor were plastered with blood and organs, both human and dinosaur.

The tables and chairs had been overturned in the skirmish. A large raptor lay stretched over a row of tables, a man's leg dangling from his mouth, and a hand protruding from the gash that stretched across the creature's throat. It looked as if the victim and made one last chance to escape from the inside out, but they never quite made it.

Further along, a long smear of blood led to the disembowelled bodies of two soldiers, whose gore-smeared faces were unrecognizable to Abbott.

Behind him, a chair clattered and he spun around, his weapon ready to fire.

"Sorry," Caroline said for the second time, not realizing in that moment how close she came to being shot for the second time in a matter of minutes.

"Jesus Christ," Abbott yelled, his voice echoing around the slaughterhouse that had once been a bustling canteen.

"Sorry, I slipped." Caroline looked near to tears as she stood, arms folded, hugging herself.

"Here, take this, if anything moves that isn't one human, shoot it," Abbott said, handing his pistol over to Rob.

"I've never fired a gun." Rob shook his head but took the weapon regardless.

"It's like driving an automatic car. Just point it and pull the trigger," Abbott said, turning to pick up a blood-covered M16 from the floor. "Stay together, watch the door; we don't want to get trapped. I'm going to the back, there has to be someone alive in here."

Abbott left the pair and made his way towards the back of the canteen and the kitchen area.

Blood covered the floor as far as he could see. A severed arm lay to the left, a pistol still clutched in the death grip.

Shotgun shells lay further ahead, and the torn open body of Sergio Diaz. His body had bene torn open, leaving a hole the size of a dinner plate clean through his chest. Ribs and organs had been crushed and torn free, devoured by the hungry mouth of the dead dinosaur that lay to the left. A chewed-up shotgun lay beneath its head, the top portion of which was missing.

In the kitchen area of the canteen, the carnage continued. Two members of the Black Arrow team lay in a tangled mass of broken and bloody limbs. Their bodies entwined with the stinking, offal-leaking corpse of a raptor-like dinosaur. They looked like a twisted vision of a great old god, pulled through the veil and into the world of men, only to perish before its reign could begin.

"Chris?" a weak-sounding voice called out.

"Dave?" Abbott recognized the voice and turned to look deeper into the kitchen.

"Chris, help me," the voice croaked again.

Moving slowly, he stepped over the contorted monstrosity that lay on the floor. The meaty pile was a pulverized mound of flesh, turned inside out by the stream of hot lead that spewed from the barrels of death-dealing M16s. Two more rifles lay in the pool nearby in a pool of innards.

Following the trail of devastation, Chris moved behind the central island and there, lying on the floor in a puddle of his own filth, lay his roommate Dave Power.

"Chris … hey, buddy," Dave stuttered, looking up from the floor. "Nasty buggers those things."

Dave was British by birth, and while he had lived away from his fatherland the majority of his life, his accent and mannerisms were impeccably British by nature.

Even as he sat, covered in death sweats, his innards cradled in his arms like a child, he remained proper.

Chris knew his friend was dead. Dave knew it too, and so Christopher crouched down and took his friend's hand. "Rest soft, buddy," he whispered.

Dave wept and gasped as the final moments of his life faded away.

"We need to move," Christopher said as he strode from the kitchen. He held two M16s and had another slung over his shoulder.

"I don't want one," Caroline said as he thrust the rifle into her hands.

"I don't care. Point it, use it, we need to get out of here," Christopher said, leading the way out of the kitchen.

"Out of the kitchen?" Caroline asked.

"Out of the building," Christopher answered.

"But, the storm … those things." Caroline stopped walking.

"Those things are in here too," Christopher yelled, his patience snapping. "They are in here, and they are eating everybody, so yes, we need to get out. We need to make our way to the back island. The security building."

Caroline opened her mouth to speak, but Rob stepped up and pulled her close to him. "It's going to be fine, but we need to listen to him. Come on, let's go." His words were gentle.

Caroline nodded, her hand finding Rob's. She squeezed hard and did not let up even as they started following Christopher, who strode through the halls, his rifle raised, and tucked into his shoulder. He did not slow down, but kept a watch on the pair to ensure they kept up the pace.

"We need to stop by the lab," Rob said, as they finally caught up with Christopher.

"Nope, no can do. Nobody is answering on the radio. We are getting out of here," he answered without hesitation.

"Listen, we need to get to the lab," Rob insisted.

"You don't get it. Those things, they are killing machines. The ultimate predator. We need to get out and call for help." Christopher flashed an angry glare back at Rob.

"The lab is sealed. They are safe. Those things—"

"If the lab is sealed, they are safe. We are not," Christopher snapped, whirling around on the pair.

"And taking us outside is going to help us on that front?" Rob raised his voice in response. "I know you are just as freaked out about this as we are. Those guys back there, they were your friends, I get that. But you need to shut up and listen to me, goddammit. That lab is a sealed environment. If the power holds out, we can slip inside and wait the storm out. Who knows, maybe those things will leave too. Either way, come morning, the weather will clear, and we will have one less thing to be terrified about."

Out of breath and panting, Rob stepped back down and stared at Christopher.

For a few moments he said nothing, but a roar echoing down the hallway changed things.

"Fine, but we'd better hurry," Christopher said, the anger and fight leaving his face.

CHAPTER 15

"Something has these guys all riled up," Dr. Matthews said as he draped a cloth over the final cage.

"They are still animals. Maybe there is something in the air, you know, a rain storm or something," Nattie answered, staring at the cages.

"I don't know, but it had better not be a reaction to the strain, because we would be back to square one again," Wesley Matthews said, standing with his hands on his hips.

"Don't be such a downer, Wesley," Nattie said.

Dr. Matthews was the resident pessimist in the group. Every setback or delay was a potential nightmare of epic proportions.

"I'm telling you, Natalie, I have bad feeling about this." He looked at her, his face set like stone.

Nattie hated being called by her full first name, but when it came to Wesley, he refused to use anything but. A prim and proper Englishman, he thought that nicknames and shortened versions of names were an affront to common decency.

Nattie went to answer him, but at that moment, the power went out.

The lab was plunged into darkness. Everybody froze. The sealed lab hid the noise and distractions of the outside world perfectly. As such, the group found themselves plunged into an unknown and unexpected void.

Nobody screamed, but the collective round of gasps and the silence that followed made the darkness even more uncomfortable and alienating.

"The back-up generator should have kicked in by now," Wesley said after a time.

"I'm sure it will, but these things take time. Without power, it is probably a manual process," Nattie offered.

A light appeared, a small rectangle of light, shining from the other side of the lab. Nattie recognized it and followed suit. Pulling her phone free from her pockets, she found the flashlight app and a fresh beam of light filled the world.

One by one, everybody did the same, and the lab came back into view. The concentrated beams of light gave the scene a menacing look, like the lair of some mad scientist rather than a government-run research institution.

After a few minutes, there was a strange humming sound and with a flicker, the lights came back on.

"Guess they got it up and running," Harriet Jones spoke up. She and her partner, Lana Hepburn, were pressed against one another in the rear corner of the room.

"I hope we did not lose any data," Remi Henry spoke, his heavy accent even thicker after the shock of the power cut.

"Yes, it is automatically updated to the cloud, and saved to three different server locations," Nattie answered.

"Yes, but what about the other work? Are you backing that up, or did it happen to slip your mind that there are some things being done in this lab that does not belong in the cloud?" Henri asked. He was a passive-aggressive man whose voice often turned into a whine. Nobody took him seriously; it was just his way. He meant no harm, and that only served to make his mannerisms comical.

"I know, Remi, I have everything saved and backed up to external drives in my office. We are fully covered," Nattie answered.

"Good, I would hate for all of this to have been for nothing. I have missed almost the entire series of Desperate Soccer Moms, and I don't trust my housekeeper to record it every week, like I instructed." Having spoken his mind, Remi turned and returned to his work. "Oh, this dim light is going to play havoc with my eyes. I feel a migraine coming on already."

The door to the lab opened with a rush of air. Everybody turned to look, their senses still on high alert.

It took a moment for them to recognize Rob and Caroline. They looked different.

"What is that?" Lana Hepburn asked, pointing to a thick strand that dangled over Rob's shoulder.

Rob looked and brushed it off. A dark red smear was left behind.

"Dinosaur intestine," he answered matter-of-factly.

"Dinosaur what now?" Nattie asked.

"Yes, there has been an accident, a breach," Caroline blurted out, causing an instant spread of panic through the group.

"Everybody calm down," Chris Abbott addressed the group, walking forward. "There is no reason to panic. Yes, there has been an incident here in the main building, but it is under control. As long as we stay here, then there is nothing to worry about. I promise."

He finished speaking, and a beach-ball-sized hole appeared in the wall. An explosion of bricks, mortar, and dust filled the air. Rain and wind whipped through the room, alerting everybody for the first time to the storm that raged.

Another impact tore through a second patch of wall. Now people began to scream.

"Everybody get back," Christopher Abbott called, moving through the lab, his rifle raised.

He trained his sights on the hole, which stood the size of a small child after the repeated assault from outside.

"What's happening?" Lana cried out

"Oh my God," Harried screamed as a large lizard-like head forced its way through the gap. Despite the size of the hole, the creature's head did not fit through fully.

A burst of gunfire echoed around the room. Bloody clouds puffed into the air like exploding spores as the hot, lead slugs penetrated the thick flesh of the creature's skull.

Inside the lab, wind whipped, blowing the covers from the cages. The small creatures threw themselves around the cages in a frenzy.

Their reveal caught Christopher's eye, and in that moment, the wounded beast got away, disappearing into the darkness of the storm.

"What is happening?" Wesley asked, grabbing Christopher by the shoulders.

Thunder rumbled and lightning struck, connecting with something in the compound's main yard.

"Oh God, we are all going to die," Remi called as he ducked down to hide behind the central lab area.

"We're not going to die, we just need to rethink our options," Abbott replied, his voice gruff and determined.

"What's your plan?" Rob asked. He and Caroline stood together just behind Christopher.

"Damned if I know," he replied in a whisper, turning to face the pair, a slight trace of a smile on his face.

The island decided for them when a crash saw the damaged rear wall collapse inwards on itself. A hulking, horned beast the size of a truck charged into the lab, smashing and crashing its way through everything.

Everybody screamed, Christopher fired his M16 until the magazine clicked empty. Rob raised his gun to fire, but in doing so, forgot to remove the safety.

The triceratops gave a roar as blood dribbled from its flank where the bullets found their mark.

"Get down," Nattie called as the immense body of the creature spun around. The tail crashed through the walls of her office, smashing the remaining lab equipment that had not already been destroyed.

"Shoot it," Remi screamed as the desk he cowering behind disappeared. "Shoot it now."

Rob shook the rifle in his hands, as if the motion would be enough to prompt the tool into working.

"Give that here," Christopher said, pulling the rifle from the young man's hand.

Firing a burst, he cursed aloud as the triceratops changed back out into the storm, leaving behind it a gaping hole in the wall that exposed the group to the violence of the elements and the mercy of the beasts that lived on the island.

"Lana, Lana?" Rob heard Harriet crying above the din of the storm.

"Is everybody alright?" Nattie asked, limping over the debris to join Rob, Caroline, and Christopher.

"Where's Lana?" Harriet asked.

"Where is Wesley?" Caroline added, looking around.

The rain whipped into the lab, soaking them to their skin in a matter of moments as they scurried about, moving piles of broken lab equipment, dry wall sheets, bricks and mortar.

Nattie found Wesley. His body lay beneath a pile of rubble, crushed by the weight which fell on him as the dinosaur charged into the building. His eyes stared at Nattie, glazed over by death, but wide with fright nonetheless.

Harriet and Rob found Lana, alive, but just barely, her wounds already sealing her fate. Her legs had been crushed by the stampeding triceratops, squashed to the point of bursting, like a trodden-on piece of fruit.

Her pale skin turned white with shock, and she stuttered her words, speaking a stream of nonsensical syllables as her brain attempted to process everything going on around her.

She died with a whimper, a dribble of dark red blood flowing from the corners of her mouth.

"We need to move," Christopher said, his attention not on the scene around him, but on the bigger picture at large.

"I'm not leaving her," Harriet snapped in response.

"If you don't want to end up like her, then you will have to. I don't want to be the hard ass, that was Hunter. Those things killed him. They would pick us apart like we did not even exist." Christopher knew people were scared, and he understood that they were not trained soldiers. Even he found himself struggling to maintain his composure. Had he been alone then, he was certain it would be a different story.

"What do you suggest?" Rob stepped up to ask.

"There is a shelter on the next island over. If we could get up to the walkways ..." Chris paused, to gather his thoughts.

"What if those things are already up there?" Remi asked. "They will eat us like candy."

"They are not here exploring. They are machines. Made for the kill. They are hunting, nothing more than that. If we beat them up there, we can seal it off," Christopher reasoned, hoping to avoid a drawn-out debate on the subject.

"How do we know the same has not happened over there?" Charlotte asked with a whisper.

"Well, then we are royally fucked, so let's worry about that if it happens." Chris felt his patience running thin.

The adrenaline was starting to wear off, and the terror at their situation threatened to cripple him if he took too long to think about things.

"But what—?" Remi began.

"We don't try, we die here, in this lab. Don't you understand? We need to try something. Now we can think as we move, but we are not staying here any longer," Chris yelled, his voice rising above the storm, his anger cancelling out their trepidation. "Now help me get this door open."

The emergency power still controlled the door, but it had been damaged during the initial assault from the triceratops. Rob gripped the dented door and pushed with all his body weight. His sweat-drenched hands made it difficult to find purchase on the rain-slicked door. Twice his grip had failed, his hands slipping. The second time, he sliced open his thumb in a wound almost identical to Caroline's, which remained wrapped in the makeshift bandage Rob had applied.

"Come on, try one last time," Christopher said as he pulled on the door.

It creaked and groaned, opening a fraction. Rob grunted, pushing from his knees. The door opened with a sudden spring.

Rob caught himself before fell on his face. He stood up, looked in the doorway, and screamed as the raptor's mouth opened in what he swore to be a grin.

The head exploded a moment later, and Rob's world descended into an ear-splitting wail as the sound of the rifle's automatic fire deafened him momentarily.

The raptor fell to the floor, its skull cracked open like a coconut. Behind it, however, more things moved in the shadows.

"Close the damned door," Christopher called, putting his weight into pushing the reinforced door shut again.

They didn't make it.

The next dinosaur to attack them hit the door just before it closed.

The creature stood as tall as a man, but its head was covered in spikes. They rose from either side of its skull and the underside of its jaw. They even curled outside from its nose. To look at it, Rob thought dragon, but he did not take the time to consider it any more than that. He turned and ran.

Christopher opened fire. Rob grabbed Caroline and pulled her away from the door, turning to face the carnage. Bullets spewed from the M16 and pummelled the spiny creature's face. Even with its jaw blown half off and his throat all but slashed, it continued to fight. Blood sprayed from its wounds until almost empty, collapsing on the raptor, successfully blocking the exposed doorway.

It proved to be a temporary reprieve, for a number of snouts appeared, forcing their way through the doorway, snapping at the air. They scratched and clawed at the bodies on the floor as they tried to force their way towards the fresh meat in the lab.

"I'm out. We need to move," Christopher called.

"Where?" Henri screamed.

"Outside, now move." Christopher ran, hustling the others along.

Rob followed, with Caroline clinging to him. They ran out of the lab, sprinting through the triceratops-shaped hole in the wall and out into the whirling, snarling midnight of the storm.

Thunder roared, and even the lightning seemed to be losing the battle against the darkness.

Rob squeezed his hand around Caroline's. He called to her but his voice was drowned out by the sounds of Mother Nature's anger to the point that even he could not hear it.

The compound, the island, nothing existed. The storm created a void, a space of deafening noise and violence that permeated an ever-powerful gust of wind.

Rob had no idea where the others were. He thought he saw a flash of gunfire in the distance, but he could not be sure.

"Keep moving. Stay close to me," Rob yelled, unsure if anybody could hear him.

The ground rumbled. Rob caught movement in the darkness. All around them, the island had come to life.

Something roared, a high-pitched, powerful sound. It cut through the storm, identifiable as another sound within the thunderous din. The wind changed, becoming a downward force. Unseen wings beat against them. Something jabbed at Rob. He swatted out in the darkness. Pain engulfed him and suddenly, the ground was gone.

He felt Caroline pulling him as pain exploded in his right arm. He could feel blood flowing as whatever latched on to him tried to take flight.

The air around Rob caught fire. Caroline fell away. Something rushed passed him. Bullets. Someone was shooting at him, at the creature attacking him. Blood sprayed in his face, and the pressure on his arm was gone.

Suddenly, Rob was in mid-air. He fell to the ground. Unable to see anything clear in the darkness, he could not brace himself for the impact. He hit the ground, and after a flash of lightning at the moment of impact, everything went dark.

CHAPTER 16

Johan Krauss sat in his library, musing over the mounds of paperwork that had accumulated over the years.

Many might consider the old man a hoarder, but he knew better. Hoarders never knew what to get rid of and so kept everything. Johan was different. He knew what to keep, and he got rid of everything else.

Paperwork was important. The right paperwork was priceless. Over the years, he had developed a fine art out of conducting his business practices, each one of them appeared fully legitimate. Many were, becoming the means by which he acquired knowledge for his other business dealings. That was where the line between right and wrong became blurred. Those situations called for the right paperwork to be kept and the selected right paperwork to be filed.

Black Arrow Security had many layers, many levels. Only Johan, and a few trusted comrades, men who had shared the foxhole with him, knew the full extent of the company's reach. It was a secure empire he had built, and everything was filed away with the tax authorities, in some form or another.

Yet something was troubling him.

There was more going on out on the islands than his secret allies in the US government were letting on. While he had no right to demand full disclosure on the basis of his curiosity, his men were dying, and that did not sit well with him.

Until now, all of Johan's attempts to contact Director Werkhoven had resulted in shut doors, varying messages depending on which level of security he reached. The excuses ranged from him being in a meeting, to being out of the country, for business and pleasure, depending on the call he made. One person even claimed that he did not exist and tried to convince Johan of this.

With each dead end he found, Johan's frustrations grew. Three of his men were dead, and while everything had a simple explanation, it did not sit right with him.

Johan learned at an early age to trust the feeling in his gut. It never failed him, and now, it screamed that something was wrong.

Reading through the paperwork again, a coffee in one hand, and a cigar smouldering within reach of his other, his head starting to spin as the words shifted on the page, forming a jumble of nonsense.

Johan did not know the last time he slept. Two, maybe three days ago. When his instincts tugged at his subconscious, he was but a slave to their voice. Draining his cup, he filled it again and returned to his studies.

The first death had been an accident, explained and accounted for. The man's family had been informed, and a generous donation had been made into their bank account; more than enough to set them up for life.

The next three had been outside of the compound. Johan trusted the reports, and while everything seemed unfortunate, he found nothing damning in the statements. These families also received notification and reimbursement for their losses.

Johan was not necessarily one of the good guys, but he was not a complete monster. He knew that those that worked for the Black Arrow group were, for the most part, hard-working men and women.

What troubled Johan was how little he knew about the experiments the Americans were conducting on the islands. He had received mixed signals from his men. They also knew very little about the islands.

The last communication with anybody had been a week ago. A long-standing agreement with his teams around the world was a twice-weekly check-in. Johan did not oversee each and every one, but received feedback on them.

The last word from the islands had been that a storm threatened to hit them that afternoon. Since then, it had been radio silence, as if they no longer existed.

Finally, as the clock hit four in the morning, Johan closed the file and placed his head on the desk, just to rest for a second.

When the feeling of queasiness had passed, he stood and picked up the telephone.

"Good morning, come to my office, I have a job for you," he spoke into the receiver.

Johan rarely introduced himself on the phone. When he called someone, they knew who it was calling. Johan liked control. He controlled everything in his life, even the way his telephone conversations played out.

***

It took three days before Amare and Clarke made it to California. Combined, they had circumnavigated the globe in order to answer the call of their employer.

Now they stood in his study, surrounded by literature and paintings. Tall ceilings and long windows were framed by heavy drapes. The room was old school and did not suit either man's taste, but neither could deny that their boss belonged in such a room. It fit his character perfectly.

"Thank you for joining me, gentlemen." Johan's voice carried through the room, as he walked up behind them. "Please, don't stand on ceremony here. Take a seat."

"It must be important if you're gonna buzz us from across the globe," Clarke spoke, his Australian accent stronger than ever.

"It is, and I need men I can trust," Johan answered, getting down to business.

"Tell us," Amare spoke, his gruff voice serious and curt.

"There is something wrong on the islands. I have no had contact with the team there for ten days." Johan paused to take a drink from his coffee.

"You think something happened to 'em?" Clarke asked.

"I don't know. Our friends within the US government have disappeared and are refusing to give me anything to go on." Johan sat back in his chair, relaxing a little as he spoke with his most trusted hands.

"I told you not to trust the Yanks," Clarke answered quickly.

"I don't care about them. There are other countries, other governments that will see the benefit of working for me," Johan answered, lighting a cigar.

"Then why do you want us?" Amare asked, his grumpy persona no less than what either man had expected.

"I want you to go back, to head to the islands, find out what is going on. There are secrets within those compound walls, and I want you to find out what it is." Johan looked from one man to the other.

Neither showed any sign of hesitance. Neither man would admit fear, especially not in the company of one another. That was why they made such an effective team. While they would never be best friends, there was a level of respect that could not be broken.

"What sort of team are we taking in?" Clarke asked, sitting forward in the leather armchair.

"I want something small. Get in, get out. I'm talking covert. We will drop you outside the compound, and I want you in and out before anybody know what has happened," Johan said.

"Even our own guys?" Clarke asked, his interest in the operation piqued.

"Even our own guys. I don't want anybody to know. Who knows what is going on." Johan sat back, allowing his words to sink in.

"You don't trust them, the Americans, or the men you put there," Amare spoke, as blunt as ever. In all the years, he had worked for Johan, all of the meetings and discussions he had been privy to, tact was something he never developed.

"I think those islands are more dangerous than we thought. Isolation like that, it can do funny things to a man, and no, I don't trust the Americans as far as I can spit." Johan smiled. "Take three guys, you choose. Godfrey will fly you in. You will make the jump and rendezvous on the third island. Use the walkway, and the chopper will pick you up from the roof. Got it?"

There would not be a second run through of the plan. Orders like this were given once, and once only. The two men nodded, looked at each other, and glared. It was as close to a handshake as they would get, but the meaning behind it was the same.

CHAPTER 17

The ride was smooth, and the helicopter close to silent. The men on board knew what they needed to do, and none of them were there for their conversational skills.

Clarke and Amare sat behind the cockpit, staring down the belly of the chopper. A new state-of-the-art design, it was a quiet ride.

The three men they had chosen sat along the wall. Their faces were blacked out with camo cream, their expressions set with stony determination.

Dennis Blankenstijn was a small man with a crop of messy blond hair. His green eyes seemed to glow in the darkness of the cabin. Despite his small stature, he was as ferocious as any man twice his size. His skills in hand-to-hand combat were second to none. Clarke chose him for that reason. The pair went back a long way. Having been through hell together on an ill-fated mission in the jungles of Cambodia, they had remained in contact ever since.

Beside him, Marcus Davies sat staring out of the open chopper door. Strong as an ox and bull-headed, he was a force to be reckoned with. Once he got on the ground, he became a juggernaut. All they needed to do was point him in the right direction, and he would just not stop. Armed with more weapons than a person could physically carry, and what could only be described as a fetish for grenades, he was everything you would not want on a covert mission. Loud, and proud of it, Marcus did not care for the subtle approach, and never would.

The third member of the team, hand-picked by Amare, was a grizzled, scarred man by the name of Luther. He had no second name, at least not that he shared with anybody. He was missing two fingers on his right hand, and his face and body were badly scarred. Nobody asked him about them. Somebody did once, and Luther cut his throat in front of the group. A terrifying man, Clarke did not like having him around, but Amare insisted, and with his pick already included, he could not say no. A lethal shot, Luther could shoot the asshole of a gnat in mid-jump from five hundred yards.

For all intents and purposes, the group did not belong together, yet they would have to work together in order to get the information they needed.

"We jump in five minutes." Clarke gave the order. Nobody answered, or even looked his way in recognition.

"Are you seeing this, mate?" Clarke whispered to Amare.

"Yes," he answered.

"It's dark. That compound should have the perimeter lights running twenty-four seven," Clarke said, not in question but to give voice to his thoughts.

Amare said nothing, but his eyes were fixed on the shark shadows beneath them. His knuckles whitened as he clutched his rifle.

The jump was easy, but the darkness was disorienting.

The men landed within a small radius of one another, but the lack of perimeter lighting had not featured in their plans.

"Regroup, we move as a unit. I'll lay down the marker. Reach it and wait for my signal to move," Clarke whispered into his radio. He pulled a thermal generator out of his pocket, placed it on the ground, and took a step back.

The device would allow the other members of the group to find his location, but would also show up on any sensors running inside the compound.

Clarke knew the risk of such a move, but so far, nothing had gone according to plan with the island. He knew first-hand what creatures lived there and would rather answer questions of fellow Black Arrow employees than wander aimlessly into the den of God knows what.

Amare arrived at the meeting spot. Clarke signalled him from his hiding spot, and the man came, moving like a ghost through the trees. Next came Blankenstijn, who held a knife in both hands, ready for anything. Clarke had given him the nickname of wolverine many years earlier. The man always seemed to produce a blade at the right moment.

Davies came soon after, his movement through the trees noisy and attention grabbing. He moved with a slow, brashness that only came from years of being the top dog in any situation.

The four men waited for Trevor, but when he did not show after a few minutes, they agreed to move in search of him. They would need his good eyes to watch the guard posts while Dennis scurried over the wall with Clarke. Amare and Davies would stay back and lay down covering fire if all things went to shit.

"This is where I came down," Dennis whispered, pointing to a spot to their left. "I dumped my chute in a hollow stump ten paces to the further back."

"Did you see Trevor coming down out of the helo?" Davies asked, his eyes sweeping the darkness for any signs of trouble.

"Yes, he jumped before me. I saw him coming down, must have been, well, due east from here," Clarke answered. "He can't be far."

They carried on searching a few minutes, wandering further from the main compound.

"I've got something," Dennis spoke up. The men had spread out through the trees, sweeping the forest like a team of volunteers looking for evidence.

Dennis bent down and picked up a knife. A distinctive weapon, they had all watched Trevor sharpening it, slow and methodically during their flight.

"There's blood on it," Dennis said. "There's blood everywhere, fucking litres of the stuff."

As if to prove his point, Dennis stamped up and ground on the wet floor, making the dirt squelch beneath his feet.

"A big ass storm just moved through. Probably got the natives restless. If one of those things came across Trevor, it will be regretting it right about now, that's for damn sure," Clarke said, taking the Rambo-style hunting knife and sliding it into the back of his pack. "Let's spread out, and stay alert. Those things could be everywhere."

They found Trevor a few moments later. Half of him at least. His body had been split through the middle, the skin sliced open and pulled apart. His upper body lay in a twisted heap, his skull sliced through the middle. A trail of still warm intestines dangled from his body like tentacles.

Amare bent down and felt the pile of innards. "Warm. Whatever did this is still here." No sooner had he spoken than something came crashing through the trees.

In the dark, nobody got a good look at what attacked them. The dinosaurs were small, not much larger than chickens. They moved liked greased pigs, slipping through the group of men without so much a noticing they were there.

"What were they running from?" Dennis asked, curious.

"I don't think we want to know," Clarke answered, just as the ground started to rumble. "Run."

The group set off. Marcus stood his ground for a moment, but turned to run when the creature burst into view, with what remained of Trevor embedded onto the curved spines that extended out from either side of its head. The size of a large bull, with tough, plated skin, it charged at them, grunting as it closed the ground.

"We need to head to the compound. Our cover is blown. Head to the front gate. They will have to let us in," Clarke ordered as they moved.

"What is that thing?" Davies asked. He turned and fired on the move. The bullets bounced off the creature's horned shoulder plates without so much as slowing it down.

"Don't know, don't fucking care, mate," Clarke answered.

The group tore through the trees, stumbling in places, leaping over the debris they caught sight of in time. The compound came into view, but Clarke felt the momentary hope of respite fade away. The compound was in ruins. It looked as if a war had been waged there.

The wall was broken in several places. Whatever caused the damage charged through the electrified fence without care or caution. Inside the compound, the main building was a burned-out shell of what it had once been.

"Don't stop. Get inside, spread out. There is a corridor to the left and to the right. Split up. Davies. You packing something good, mate?" Clarke asked.

"You know it," Marcus answered, pulling a grenade from his trousers like a magician pulling a coin from behind some kid's ear.

"Good. Wait for it, and then blow that fucker away." They reached the main building and split.

Clarke moved to the right, along with Blankenstijn and Amare, while Davies spun to the left. He stopped and the turned, the grenade armed and ready to the throw.

The beast charged full speed into the building, crashing through the fractured remains. The walls crumbled beneath the weight of its charge, and it soon powered its way from sight, driving deeper into the building.

"This place won't stay standing for very long," Blankenstijn said as the walls began to groan around them.

"This is fucked up. Davies, take care of that thing. Amare, we need a way out." Under most circumstances, Amare would hate being bossed around, especially by Clarke, but even a man such as him understood that survival became the sole important thing to consider.

Davies moved toward the path carved by the beast. The creature had turned, and much like a bull in a Spanish ring, as it turned, it prepared to charge them again.

The beast ran with its head lowered to the floor, horns primed. At some point, Trevor's tattered remains had fallen free, leaving the horn blood-smeared and even more menacing.

"That's right, come on, big boy," Marcus shouted as he launched the first grenade with a strong trust of his arm.

Without waiting, he conjured another explosive, and in a fluid motion, primed the weapon and rolled it down through the building.

Turning to the others, he had time to smile before the first explosion tore the carcass of the main building apart. The blast ripped through the walls, covering the men in a shower of bricks and mortar dust.

The first explosion tore the creature apart. Its belly burst and hindquarters blossomed outward like a blooming flower. The rear legs became meaty stumps, blood and bone crushed and fused together like some hideous, skinless sculpture. Blood splattered in all directions, but the beast did not stop. Its powerful front legs continued to drag its mutilated body forward.

The second grenade detonated and blew the thing's head apart. The two cranial mounted horns flew to the left and the right, spinning like death stars launched in a final attempt to fight for survival.

The creature's hulking body came to a rest, collapsing inward upon itself. Meat, blood, and brain juices covered the floor and walls of the hall, and the aroma of roasted meat filled the wrecked building.

"You want to try some?" Amare said, prodding the cooked flesh as they all stood around the beast.

"Fuck off with that," Clarke spat in instant response.

"You like a barbeque, no?" Amare said, cracking a joke for the first time in all the years Clarke had known him.

"Well, didn't you pick a perfect fucking time to find a sense of pissin' humour," Clarke added, watching the cold-blooded African man. He regarded him with an increased trepidation, given how calm he seemed to be under the circumstances.

"What do we do now, Skippy?" Blankenstijn asked Clarke.

"We get the fuck out of this place. This building ain't going to survive long. Who knows what else is out there. We are sitting ducks, and sure as fuck are not prepared to wage a war. The mission was in and out. That's what we do." Clarke was resolute in his words. He hated the island, always had, and he did not plan on spending any longer on any of them than he needed to.

The men moved through the building together, their weapons raised and ready for a fight. They didn't talk. They watched and studied every nook and cranny.

Power cables hung loose from the gaping holes blown into the ceiling. A desk lay suspended by one leg above their heads. The computer that belonged to it lay shattered on the floor.

A steady tick and hiss echoed around them. The building was dying, bleeding out, while they wandered around in awe of the damage.

The stairwell was still intact, but only just. Moving slowly, they reached the second floor, and started to head towards the walkway that would bring them to the third island.

"Guys, hold up," Clarke said as they moved through the building. An enormous hole had been torn into the wall, and from the upper level, they looked out over the jungle.

"We need to move," Amare said, his good humour of earlier long gone.

"No, look." Clarke pointed out into the darkness.

"I don't see anything," Davies said dismissively.

"That's because you're a blind dingo," Clarke snapped. "Take a proper fucking look."

The four men stood and stared at the orange glow lighting up a patch of the darkness.

"What is that?" Dennis asked.

"I think it is the remainder of the people stationed here. I don't know how it happened, but they got chased away by the creatures on this island." Clarke turned to face the others.

"Good for them. We got what we needed to get. Now we leave," Amare said, the cold-hearted killer back in control.

"You can't be serious." Clarke looked at the man with open eyes.

"This was not a rescue mission. In and out. We came, we got in, and now we get out. It's simple." Amare turned and walked away.

"No, we are going to help them. They are alone out there, with these ... these ... dinosaurs," Clarke spat the word, which felt strange and stupid on his tongue, especially when used in the context of a real, viable threat.

"Bollocks to that. I love a good scrap, but I'm not getting involved in some rescue mission. That's not what I'm getting paid for," Marcus snapped, moving to follow Amare over the walkway.

Clarke and Dennis stood side-by-side. They looked from one another, to the figures disappearing down the walkway, and over to the orange glow from what he could only assume was the survivor's fire.

"You are really going to walk away?" Clarke called after the pair and set off in a run after the pair.

Reaching the two, he grabbed Amare by the shoulders, spinning the man around. "I never took you for a coward," Clarke roared at him.

Amare said nothing, but his balled fist connected with Clarke's jaw in a spurt of motion so fast it belied belief. Stung by the blow, Clarke shook it off, much to Amare's surprise.

The Australian threw a series of shots in response, the first one a feint, the second a tap to set up the third. His crushing blow to Amare's sternum doubled the man over.

Clark moved in closer, missing with a knee to the side of Amare's head. The African man was fast, jumping out of range and back into fighting distance in a fluid motion. Thrusting his head forward, he connected with Clarke's head, opening up a long gash in the Australian's eyebrow.

Clark let out a cry, throwing an elbow in response. Both men grappled and fell to the floor, rolling over one another.

Watching for a moment, Marcus moved to get involved and found a knife at his throat.

"Don't even think about it, buddy," Dennis growled. The knife's blade was razor sharp, drawing a pink trickle of blood along the contact point.

"Fuck you. I'm getting off this place. I don't want no part of it," Marcus said, raising his hands in submission.

He backed away and disappeared down the corridor while Amare and Clarke continued to grapple on the floor.

"Coward," Dennis said under his breath.

On the floor, Amare gained the upper hand in their fight. Clarke's bloodied face hindered his fighting abilities, and when the blade pressed against his throat, he knew to call it a day.

"You are not so tough," Amare snarled, breathing heavily. "Try it, boy, and I will gut you like a beast."

Dennis froze with his knife moving towards the feral black man. Something in the words forced Dennis's brain and preservation instincts to kick in.

"I am getting off this island. I will not risk my life for anybody that is not paying me. We did our job. I am done." His face glistened with sweat, and his wide eyes gave his face a lunatic quality.

Clarke offered no retaliation, even as Amare got off him and backed away. The Australian remained on the floor, watching to see where things would go from there.

"You are really just going to walk away?" Dennis called after the pair.

"Leave them be. They are not worth it," Clarke said, as he hauled himself back to his feet. "We have bigger problems on our hands."

As if on cue, a loud crash rang out belong them, followed by a series of cough-like barks.

"We have company." Clarke looked at Dennis.

"Great. Let's roll out the welcome wagon." Dennis patted his rifle and smiled.

"I've got a better idea." Clarke pointed to the floor where two grenades lay.

"Where did they come from?" Dennis asked, bending down to pick them up.

"Marcus must have dropped them," Clarke answered, taking one from his friend.

Below them, they could hear the creatures moving about. Their heavy footsteps crunching on the debris that littered the ground floor.

"I say we drop these bad boys, and take the emergency exit," Clarke said, bouncing the explosive up and down in his hands, as if testing the weight.

"Why the fuck not," Dennis answered.

The two men stood either side of the stairwell. They saw one of the dinosaurs moving around the wreckage. It was a mottled green colour and walked on two legs. Its tail extended out behind it, almost doubling its length. The head was small and ended in a strange hooked beak. From the short glimpse they got, fang-like teeth rose from the thing's lower jaw as an extra line of both defence and attack.

"How many are there?" Dennis asked.

"At least two by my count, but I would say more," Clarke answered, his eyes focused on the darkness. "They know we are here."

He did not have time to consider his words before the first creature leapt out of the darkness. Its jaws snapping shut in a blur of motion. A red stripe ran down either side of the beast's beak, something they had not noticed on the others in the group.

"Now," Clarke ordered, and he threw his grenade down the stairs. It bounced twice and disappeared into the darkness.

Dennis followed suit, launching his grenade so that it bounced in the opposite direction. Switching to his rifle, Clarke shot off a burst of fire that struck the leaping creature in the chest, knocking it back down the stairs.

The creature landed just as the dual explosions ripped through the lower floor. Its body caught fire and blazed for a moment before seeming to explode.

Clarke opened his mouth to give another order, but realized it was not needed. Dennis turned and ran towards their intended exit with Clarke following close behind him.

They leapt and crashed through the window as a round of unexpected secondary explosions ripped through the ground floor.

Both men landed hard on the ground. They braced for the impact, and rolled with the direction of their descent, but the ground was hard and unforgiving.

They did not have time to lick their wounds, however, as a burning figure came running from within the building. It screamed in pain, a hoarse, frantic bark, before its legs gave way and it fell to the ground. The flames continued to eat their way through its blackening flesh, the scent of its cooking meat a revolting aroma unlike anything either man had encountered before.

Beyond the creature, the building was burning, collapsing inwards on itself, the fragile skeleton unable to withstand any further attacks.

"Now what?" Dennis asked, as they stared at the burning building.

"Well, I guess we have two options," Clarke said, wincing as he popped his dislocated shoulder back into place.

The flames from the building lit up the night, granting an extended field of vision. Long shadows loomed over the courtyard. There could be no mistaking the shadow of the helicopter as it passed overhead. The group of shapes that moved to meet it, however, were something else entirely.

"What the hell?" Dennis began.

"Get down," Clarke called as the helicopter bursts into flames with a screech of twisting metal and shower of electrical sparks.

CHAPTER 18

Amare moved across the walkway without looking back. He heard the footsteps following him and knew they were only one pair. Who they belonged to made no difference to him. Sure, he had his own preferences, but they mattered little in the overall scope of things.

"So where is this chopper going to meet us?" Marcus asked, huffing slightly as he jogged to catch up.

"On the roof," Amare answered with his usual verbal economy.

"Of course," Marcus grunted.

A helipad had been built onto the top of each of the three points of the walkway, one on each of the islands. It was a security measure that Johan had insisted on.

The chopper was waiting for them, Godfrey sitting behind the controls as patient as ever. He looked over as the door opened and the two figures arrived. He had heard the gunfire and seen the explosions, his lofted position affording him a view over to the main island. He had tried to radio back to the ship that was waiting for them, but he could not get an answer. They had been assigned an encrypted channel to avoid their presence being detected by those on the island.

Godfrey had a bad feeling about what had happened to them all, given the apparent need for such force on the ground.

"Where are the others?" he asked, turning as the side door to the choppers central cabin slid open.

"They are not coming," Amare answered, scowling at the pilot.

Godfrey knew better than to question the man. Amare was insane. He could think of no other word to describe the man, and it put him on edge to have him around without Johan there. His boss seemed to have a parent-like influence of the wild African man.

"Get us in the air. We are getting out of here," Marcus added, his voice hurried.

"You got it," Godfrey replied, starting up the controls. The rotors whined into life, and with a slight shudder, as they hit high gear, they took to the skies and moved away.

Godfrey took the chopper up and over the main island. As he did, he noticed the same orange glow on the side of the volcano. He stared at it for a while, turning his bird around to get a better look.

"Hey, there are people down there," he began.

"They are as good as dead, now get us gone," Amare snarled, leaning in close as if extra emphasis on his anger was needed.

"But we can save them," Godfrey began, but a knife appeared at his throat, cutting his words off.

"We did not come here on a rescue mission. We came, we did our job, and now we leave. Fuck them." It was the longest conversation the two men had ever had, and one Godfrey was keen never to repeat.

"What's that ... holy shit," Marcus began.

The other two men turned their heads, just in time to make out the horrific sight descending on them, but with too little time to do anything about it.

The first winged creature hit them from the side. Its large body, half the size of the helicopter, crushed the side of the chopper. The metal twisted and screamed as it buckled. The spinning rotors connected with flesh, slicing through it like an oversized buzz-saw

The pteranodon's body exploded with a wet splat, blood and gore gushing against the window, pouring from the gaping wounds clawed into the bird's flank. The creature gave a cry and fell away, yanking the side plates with it.

The chopper spun, the rotors damaged from the impact. Alarms and whistles screamed for attention in the cockpit, but Godfrey could do little to quiet them.

Two more of the flying beasts hit them, one landing atop of spinning rotors. Its legs were chopped into mincemeat in seconds, sending a further shower of blood and bone into the night. The main rotor motor blew apart, igniting the blood and engulfing the helicopter before anybody could react.

The second creature crashed into the side, moving in head first, its long head and tooth-laden beak filled the cabin. Snapping and shrieking, it grabbed at Marcus, severing his leg in a single bite. Blood fountained from the wound, leaving the butch man screaming like a young girl, blood squirting from his mangled stump of a limb, spraying him up like a victim in a cheap horror movie.

Amare sat eerily calm as everything around him caught fire and died. He pulled out his hunting knife and stabbed at the creature, unleashing a frenzied attack, while never losing his calm and rational look.

Trembling, Marcus reached into his jacket and pulled out a grenade; the last one he had. Pulling the pin, he held it ready in his hand. The creature swung its head, shaking the entire chopper. Amare was thrown back, his head hitting the twisted metal wall behind him.

Snapping, the jaws closed around Marcus's waist. His skin punctured and blood filled his mouth, spewing from his throat like coppery vomit. He cried out, in rage, in fear, and in sorrow.

"Fuck you," he spat, choking on his own blood as he released his grip on the grenade.

There was a flash of light, and for a moment, the air was sucked from around them. The grenade went off and blew the rear of the helicopter apart. Flames ate the shrieking pteranodon, whose head had been all but blown apart by the blast. Blood and warm globs of semi-cooked meat flew in all direction. Marcus's body tore open like a piece of over-ripe fruit. Thick, purple stands of intestine flew from the gaping hole in his gut, dancing on the force of the blast like hypnotised cobras.

The burning shell of the helicopter spun and twisted in the air, careening into the ground with the top-mounted pteranodon fused to the still-spinning ruins of the main rotor.

It crashed in a fireball of burning fuel and dinosaur flesh, lighting up the night like a second sun.

"Now what?" Dennis asked, staring at the burning wreckage of the helicopter.

"Well, I guess we only have one option," Clarke answered, turning away from the two blazing infernos to look at the small orange spec, half buried behind the tress that marked the start of the horror-filled jungle.

CHAPTER 19

Johan moved through the large house like a ghost. He had sent his staff away. His mood was as dark as the storm sky that had overtaken the coast. Moving in from the sea, it swept over the horizon like a swarm.

Thunder rumbled and lightning lit up the ocean. The windows in the house rattled, but the state-of-the-art building could withstand even the harshest of weather conditions.

Johan had not heard from either Godfrey or Clarke. That concerned him and went some way to explaining his foul mood. Bad weather always made him temperamental, his mood reflecting the heavy atmosphere of the storm. Amare never checked in. Very much a man of his own devices, he had earned the ability to go off the grid. He would return when the job was done. Not before, and not too long after.

Clarke and Godfrey were different. Johan trusted the two men as if they were his blood relatives. They knew to check in and keep him informed. Their silence, coupled with his growing sense of unease around what the Americans were up to on the island, sat in his gut like a plateful of three-day-old sushi.

A bell sounded, echoing around the house like a shrill cry. Johan stopped his pacing, confused. Who would venture out into a storm, to visit him no less? His home was isolated, and nobody knew him. It meant that only one of a handful of people could be standing at the gate.

Moving to the security room, he looked at the screens and saw a familiar face standing by the front gate. The rain pelted, looking like static on the high-definition camera feed.

Johan paused for a moment, as an uneasy feeling formed in his gut. His hand moved to buzz the gates open, but took his time, wanting to make sure his uninvited guests got the full experience of being kept in the dark on how things were going to develop. It was a childish move, but even a man as rich as Johan could find fun in an innocent form of misery.

"I did not expect to see you hear, Director," Johan said as he opened the large heavy oak doors to his home.

Director Werkhoven stood in a rain-soaked suit. He was alone, at least; anybody that had travelled with him was keeping their distance. Johan did not, for one moment, truly believe the director was alone.

"Well, I heard that you had been looking for me. Besides, I think we need to talk," Sikke answered.

Suddenly, Johan understood why the director of the NSA was on his doorstep, alone. There was something in the man's eyes that told Johan this visit was not going to be on the record as ever having happened. He buzzed open the gate and stood by the front door, waiting.

"Come in," he said, opening the door as Sikke climbed the front steps.

"Thank you," Sikke answered, crossing the threshold with his head lowered. "I could go for a drink."

"Of course, follow me." Johan closed the door and led his guest through to the library. It was his favourite room in the house and also where he kept the really good whiskey.

They sat in silence for close to thirty minutes, each man nursing a large scotch. The sound of the storm whipping around them added an unnecessary layer of drama to the scene.

"I assume you did not just come here to drink my whiskey," Johan said once it became apparent that Sikke had no impending plans on raising his voice.

"The first thing you need to understand is that I am not here in an official capacity," Sikke said, raising his head. It may have been the shadows of the room, of the battering storm he had braved outside, but the director looked much older than the last time they were together.

His face was heavily lined with deep creases, and his eyes were surrounded by swollen bags of flesh. He looked like a man who had not slept in some time.

"I understand. After all, technically speaking, this house does not exist, and you and I do not know each other," Johan said, referring back to the basic terms of their relationship, mutually agreed upon by the pair so many years before.

Sikke didn't say anything, but gave a snorted laugh. He finished his whiskey in a single gulp and let out a sigh.

"You have probably been wondering what has been going on out there, on the islands," he spoke without raising his head.

"Well, the thoughts had crossed my mind. Especially when my men started dying," Johan answered, keeping his tone stern but bordering on disinterested. He knew the game well enough to know you never give away your hand so early.

"When we first heard about the islands, you can guess the plans we had; the possibilities."

"I've seen enough movies to know what you were thinking."

"Well, a theme park was never part of the plans, but yes, you get what I am saying," Sikke spoke, leaning into the tall-backed leather chair. "We gathered some of the finest scientific minds to those islands. We created a team of microbiologists, geneticists, and military engineers. Basically, a team with enough brain power to take over the world with the knowledge we had given them."

"You have lost contact with them," Johan interrupted, unable to help himself.

"We have not been able to make contact for about a week. We were aware of a storm that moved through the area, and since then, we have been unable to contact anybody on the island. We had a satellite focus on the area, and we have seen a lot of damage around the buildings," Sikke spoke slowly, thinking about each and every word.

"Do you think they were compromised? Knowledge of the islands was widespread, in certain circles," Johan offered, standing to refill their glasses.

"We don't know. That is why I am here. I need to ask you something." Sikke raised his head, his face set with a look of stern concentration.

"You want to know if I have anything to do with the radio silence." Johan could not help but give a derisive laugh.

"Well, I know the company you keep, and how your business works. That is why I am here off the books. I am not here on government business. You and I go back a long way—"

"Yes, we do," Johan said gruffly.

"We go way back, and in all of that time, I have never once asked you about your other business avenues. I have sat back and worked with you to combat a situation I know your company was responsible for in the first place. I know all about that thing in the Sudan, and many others like it," Sikke said, his voice raised, but not in anger.

"Maybe I underestimated you Americans." It was all Johan could think to say. For years, he had assumed his paper trail was untraceable. He considered himself a ghost.

"If you thought we would not do our homework about someone we allow to live in and profit from this country, then you were indeed wrong. Until now, we have had turned blind eyes to your dealings, because our relationship was mutually beneficial, even when you did not realize it. However, now you need to answer some very serious questions." Sikke let the threat hang in the air. He did not try to hide it, nor to soften the blow. He was there on a private matter, a cordial visit, due after so many years of cooperation, but that did not change the seriousness of the occasion.

With the tide of the meeting changed, Johan took his drink and emptied the glass in a single swallow.

"What exactly are you accusing me of?" he asked, determined to hear the man say it.

"I am not accusing you of anything. If I was, you would have a bigger problem than me drinking more of your scotch," Sikke said. "I am here to ask you, man-to-man, if you have had anything to do with the radio silence coming from the island. Did you sell us out? Plant your own men there in order to give control to some other bidder?"

With the questions asked, Johan felt a wave of relief wash over him. It was so great a feeling that he could not help but give a laugh.

"You think it is funny?" Director Werkhoven asked, his voice beginning to show signs of his growing impatience.

"No, no, Director, you misinterpret my response. I have no idea what has happened on the island. As it would happen, I too was concerned about the silence coming from that port, and sent some of my best men, my own bodyguard included, back to the island just a few days ago in order to find out what has happened there," Johan answered, studying the director's face.

The hardened gaze softened, a look of puzzlement and then intrigue appeared on his features.

"What did you find out?" he asked with genuine interest.

"That is the worrying thing. I have received no word from my men since they left the boat, and as you well know, we cannot send the boat any closer to the island given the rather territorial nature of the creatures that occupy the coastline." Johan sat.

The two men stared at each other in silence, both trying to make sense of what events were transpiring on the island.

"Do you think the island could have been infiltrated?" Sikke asked, his tone dropped down to that of a casual chat.

"Not with my men around. They would have given word, a simple signal at the very least," Johan answered with unshakable certainty. "No, my fear is that whatever has happened, is the result of what was already on the island when we arrived."

Silence fell again in the room, as around them, the howl of the wind echoed like a laugh. The hidden face of Mother Nature was mocking them.

"The storm must have damaged the power source to the fence. The dinosaurs could have infiltrated the outer compound. The structure was reinforced, but the bulk of work was concentrated on the perimeter," Johan spoke, running through possible scenarios.

"Well, if we have not heard back from your men by morning, I will order a search-and-rescue mission. We have a fleet stationed nearby, close enough to reach within a day or so," Sikke said, passing the empty glass from one hand to another.

"Are they any good?" Johan asked.

"Good enough even to work for you," Sikke replied with a smile. "Come morning, we will know."

"Why Director, are you saying we are having a, what do you call it, a slumber party?" Johan asked, rising from the chair once more.

"Well, there does seem to be an awful lot of scotch back there," Sikke answered, rising from his seat to take a closer look at the impressive library.

CHAPTER 20

The night proved to be a long and torturous experience. Once Clarke and Dennis had moved away from the edges of the former compound, and the glow cast by the trio of infernos had faded, they found the night to be a near impenetrable shade of black.

The majority of their equipment was either lost or damaged, and so they made the decision to seek shelter, and set a watch, or rather, a listen.

They found shelter up a large tree, with low-hanging branches that made for an easy climb. Clarke had a flashlight that allowed them to find their way to what they both felt was a decent height.

After both men strapped themselves against the trunk of the tree, using the webbing from their packs, and a number of vines, which wrapped their way around the tree like varicose veins, they agreed upon the watch. Clarke went first, and within minutes, he heard Dennis snoring.

The night stretched on into what felt like eternity, the sun resisting the urge to rise until the last possible moment. Through it, Clarke sat in silence. He listened as the jungle swarmed around him in an endless array of crashes and grunts. Several times, their tree shook as something moved either through the upper branches or crashed against the trunk below.

While his eyes adjusted to the dark, they never moved beyond the ability to discern the different shares of darkness that surrounded them. Clarke could no soon identify the different beasts that moved by than he could recite the words to the Estonian national anthem.

When daylight finally came, it moved in swiftly, illuminating the jungle to the point of a murky dawn. The thick canopy of trees above their heads blocked almost all direct sunlight, but allowed enough through for them to see by.

The first thing Clarke noticed were the deep grooves in the ground around the base of the tree. Long, deep, trench-like gouges had been cut into the moist earth.

The signs of a struggle were confirmed by the now tacky blood smeared over the trunk of nearby trees.

"I guess we head up the side of the volcano," Dennis said, once both men were out of the tree once more.

"Looks that way. These folks survived. It was a compound full of men like us and scientists. That's a winning combination if ever I heard one," Clarke said, dropping to his knees as he looked around, surveying the dense vegetation.

"If there is anybody left," Dennis added matter-of-factly.

"Well, I doubt these lizard bastards made a fire last night to keep themselves warm," Clarke snapped in response. "No, let's get moving. We are not alone here, and I don't want to meet whatever it is that is watching us."

As the two men moved through the jungle, the concept that they were being watched only increased, growing on Clarke like a tumour. The soft ground made for heavy walking, but the rest had done both men well, even if they had been tied to a tree branch.

They came across several other creatures as they moved, but very few paid them any mind. Those that did scurried away at the first sight of movement from the pair.

The dinosaurs ranged from creatures that looked like a scaled down model of a pig, their bodies jet black, their tusks curled to the point of being useless in a fight.

They grunted incessantly, snuffling along with their noses buried in the ground, stopping every now and then when they found a trace of whatever it was they were looking for.

Twice, they came across such creatures, and each time, there were three of them in the group. Clarke noted it in his brain should anything happen, but the creatures had not once acknowledged their presence let alone shown any signs of aggression.

As they drew closer to the volcano, the ground beneath their feet changed. The mud hardened and turned stony. Tree roots rose from the ground, trip hazards just waiting to fell any beast that came by.

The plants and ferns that had been so thick and lush a few meters before stopped suddenly. The change in terrain made for easier walking, and while the pair's speed increased, it was not for long, as the heat of the day had them both drenched in sweat and panting in no time.

"What the hell do you think did this?" Dennis asked.

They had stopped to rest, leaning against a large tree. Above their heads, at least two and a half meters above the ground, a series of deep gouges at least an inch deep had been cut into the hardwood tree.

"I have no idea, but I don't think we really want to find out," Clarke said, sparing no more than a short glance up at the wounds scythed into the trunk. "How are you doing for ammo?"

Dennis checked his rifle. "I'm down to my last clip for the M16. I've got two dozen in the Glock and, well, my blades can go all day and all night."

"Yeah, well I hope we never get close enough to need hand-to-hand skills," Clarke answered.

"How about you?" Dennis asked, turning his back on the tree.

"I've got a half a clip loaded, another one in my pockets. A full Glock and a grenade," Clarke replied, reeling off his numbers without hesitation or double checking. "It's not going to be enough."

"What won't be?" Dennis asked as he cleaned one of this hunting knives on the thigh of his trousers.

Clarke didn't answer. His eyes were focused on the trees. He caught sight of movement, but it had been too quick for his eyes to focus.

Slowly, his hand crept down his flank towards his hip, where he unclipped the Glock he had holstered there. He moved slowly, not wanting to spook whatever was watching him.

With his fingers hooked around the butt of the Glock, he heard the delicate swoosh of a knife being removed from its sheath. Dennis had spotted them too.

The shadows moved again as something darted from behind one tree to another. It was small, crouched down low to the ground.

Clarke followed the movement, the sweat covering his body turning cold as he focused his vision.

Behind him, Dennis moved, turning away. His attention was caught by something else. They were surrounded. It did not bode well.

It happened in a blur. Dennis moved like a ghost, charging forward. There was a grunt and a cry.

"Don't shoot, don't shoot, please God, don't shoot," the frantic, fear-laden voice called out.

Clarke cast a glance back at Dennis, taking his focus away from the watchful eyes in the trees. He saw Dennis standing with a man pinned up against a tree. The man was dirty and dishevelled. His nose was bleeding, no doubt from where Dennis struck him. His hands were raised in surrender, but Dennis still held the blade of hunting knife tightly against the stranger's throat.

Clarke looked back, caught between two choices. He could not make out the shadow anymore and knew he needed to act fast before Dennis killed an innocent man.

Turning, he directed his attention towards the pair of man. Placing his hands on Dennis's shoulder, he spoke in a whisper. "It's alright, let him go."

"You know him?" Dennis asked, not yet ready to lower the knife.

"I know his face. He worked in one of the labs," Clarke answered.

This information seemed to be enough for Dennis, who lowered but did not re-sheath his blade. "What do you think you are doing, sneaking up on people like that, squinty? You lab geeks are all clueless," Dennis snapped.

"Who are you?" the man asked, his eyes darting quickly from side to side, scanning not the two men standing before him, but rather the trees behind them.

"Name's Clarke. I worked security for Black Arrow. This here is Dennis Blankenstijn. He works security also," Clarke answered, looking over his shoulder, trying to work out if this man was seeing the same shadows he had noticed.

"Black Arrow. You must know Zippy … I mean, Abbott," the man stammered, his agitation growing.

"Christopher Abbott?" Clarke asked, intrigued by the man's behaviour.

"Yeah, that's him."

"I know him. Good man. Zippy, you say? I'll remember that," Clarke said. "And you are?"

"God, he's going to kill me when he finds out I told you. I'm Rob, Rob Reddan. We really need to move now," he said, the words hurried to the point of being slurred.

"Why, what's out there??" Dennis asked, catching himself too late.

"Oh believe me, Dennis, there are worse things than dinosaurs on this island." There was a cool, calm, terror in Rob's words that even Clarke felt a cold shiver tumble down his spine.

Neither man offered any challenge when Rob stepped away from the tree, nor did they flinch when he pulled a pistol from the waistband of his trousers.

"Ain't you a regular gangster," Dennis said with a smile.

"Follow me, and try to keep up," Rob replied, his character changing with his position amongst the Black Arrow men confirmed.

The trio moved through the trees. To their left, a large, dome-headed creature crashed clumsily through the trees. Its armour-plated back made it look like a cross between a giant turtle and a hippopotamus.

"Don't worry about that thing. Stupid as they come, placid too. All it does it wander around looking for food. There's a whole family of them that live in this part of the wood," Rob spoke without slowing. "We need to move fast, those things have kept their distance for now, but we don't want to linger."

"You just said that those things were not anything to worry about," Dennis chimed in.

"Not those things. I'm talking about the vicious creatures that have been following us since we first met," Rob replied, once again not slowing his pace to offer any further explanation.

The incline grew as they started to make their way further up the volcano. The rocky ground became a scramble in some places, and while they stuck to the cover of the trees wherever possible, Clarke saw large expanses where the trees had ben felled, creating clearings and open expanses.

"We thought we had gotten lucky. We made it through the raptor zone without too much trouble, only lost one guy. We thought the dinosaurs were leaving us alone because of where we made camp," Rob said, his sentences leaving the two men feeling as if they had misheard other part of the conversation. "Then that first night they came. Bastards. You need to watch out for them. They are demons, truly they are. I've never seen anything so evil. I guess you have to be, to survive here, in this place." Finally, Rob stopped walking, and turned to face the two men. "We are here."

They looked around and saw nothing that gave an indication of shelter, although a pile of burned sticks and small bones nestled against the base of a tree told Clarke that people at least congregated in the area.

"I don't see anything—" Dennis began, but Rob cut him off by giving a shrill two-finger whistle.

The surprising loud, ear-piercing cry carried up into the trees. A few moments later, a long knotted vine fell down, unwinding from above like a rope ladder.

"You spoke too soon, mate," Clarke answered, slapping Dennis on the shoulder.

"Come on, up you go," Rob said, directing the two men towards the vine.

"What the fuck is this, some treehouse boy's club?" Dennis muttered as he grabbed the vine and started to climb.

"Second branch. Stop there and wait for me," Rob called after him. "Hurry, those things won't keep watching us forever."

Clarke turned around, surveying the trees once more. He thought he could make out the eyes watching them. At least three, by his estimation, but they were small, or at least, kept themselves low to the ground; perfect for moving through the fern-laden brush of the lower section of the island.

"Your turn, chief," Rob said to Clarke.

The Australian shimmied up the vine like a monkey, disappearing into the trees. Rob followed him, his ascent somewhat more clunky than the others, but much smoother than his initial efforts. He looked down as he climbed, watching for any sign of the creatures. In previous excursions into the forest, they had followed them back, trying to climb the rope after them. So far, they seemed to lack the skills needed to do it, but Rob was sure they were playing with them. He could not believe those creatures could survive on the island without being able to climb.

Conditions were cramped with three men, two in military gear, crouched on the same branch, but Rob managed to coil the vine up. Clarke watched, impressed at how the former lab rat wound the vine and hooked it over a splintered shard of the trunk.

"Follow me. Watch your step," Rob said, continuing to lead the group with a growing bravado.

Rob moved easily over the branch, crouched down, his arms out to either side for balance. He moved without hesitation, the only way to cross such a divide.

The tree branch came to a rocky cliff face set into the side of the volcano. A quick scramble, the least dangerous part of their journey, saw them standing in an entrance way into the volcano. Only visible from one spot on the floor, it was a miracle that they had found it.

"Welcome to paradise," Rob said with a smile.

"How many of you are here?" Clarke asked, peering into the darkness of the cave.

"There are six of us in total," a familiar voice answered. "But one is in a real bad way."

"Good God, is that you, Zippy?" Clarke answered in the dark inner shroud of the cave.

"I'm gonna kill you, Rob," Abbott growled.

"I didn't tell him. He guessed, he is Australian after all," Rob answered.

"Yeah, well, not through fucking choice," Clarke replied gruffly.

"What are you doing here?" Abbott asked, walking out of the darkness. He had a pronounced limp, and his right arm sat in a crude-looking sling. The pistol in his other hand held steady however, trained on Clarke's chest.

"We got sent in by the old man. When it went silent here, he got concerned. Didn't trust you Yanks," Clark answered with a smug smile.

"Yeah, it was hard to check in with everybody being eaten and all that." Abbott turned back towards the cave. "Come on in, we've just put on a fresh pot of coffee."

Rob chuckled as he moved into the cave with Clarke and Dennis following behind.

Clarke looked at Dennis and shook his head. The man was holding a knife, concealed against this arm. "These are friendlies. Trust me, we will need them on our side if we are going to survive this."

Dennis looked at Clarke for a moment, then his face softened and he returned the weapon to its sheath.

Moving into the cave, the darkness seemed to reduce. They followed the single track no more than ten meters deep before the cave opened up, splitting both left and right. Two small fires burned on each branch. The right hand side was empty, but the left had a crowd of people grouped together.

They turned to look at the newcomers. One look at their weapons had people ready to cheer, inwardly at least, for fear of rousing the natives. A second look, upon a closer inspection, revealed their injuries, and the lack of any long-term firepower, and their collective hearts sank.

"Rob," a young female voice called out. A petite blonde rushed away from the fire, flinging herself into the arms of the returning scout.

"You did well for yourself, mate." Clarke couldn't help but say, slapping Rob on the back with enough force to make the lab-man stumble.

"I was worried. When you didn't come back ... I ... thank God you are back." She flung herself into his arms once more.

"So, did you two come to rescue us?" a strong female voice spoke up.

From the light of the fire, Clarke identified the person, but could not make out much that than she was a confident woman. He could tell from the way she stood and how her voice carried.

"We are now," Dennis chimed in. His words spoken with a sarcastic lilt that Clarke hoped did not carry to the others.

"We ran into complications," Clarke added in swift follow up.

"Yes, we heard your stealthy approach to the compound. You were informed before arriving about the creatures that lived here, right?" Nattie Rose could not help but keep her voice loaded with venom.

Ever since the storm, things had gone from bad to worse. Her friends had been beaten, burned, and eaten alive, and the anger building up inside her needed to be released.

"Yes, ma'am," Clarke answered, adjusting his voice. He recognized the pain the scientist was going through. "I helped build it."

"You seem very proud of that fact, Mr ...?" Nattie paused.

"Clarke," he replied.

"Mr. Clarke, are you proud of what you built here?" Nattie pushed, trying to find a crack that she could attack. Her entire body tingled and felt as if it would burst if she could not release the rage-driven pressure.

"Just Clarke, ma'am. I'm a first name kind of guy." Clarke kept his tone neutral, happy that Dennis remained quiet. "I did my job, building this place. I was not the one who hired you, or ordered anybody to come here. But one thing I do know, is that there is a way out."

"A way out? You mean, off the island?" a heavily French-accented voice joined in the conversation.

"Yes, at the very least it is a safe place, fully stocked and with satellite connections to the outside world." Clarke could not be sure where the voice came from, and so kept his gaze affixed on Nattie.

"Why now? We just got this place cleaned up, and we are all having the time of lives here. A regular camping excursion," the French voice was a mixture of scorn and sarcasm. It irritated Clarke greatly.

"Listen, we are all stuck here together, and those dinosaurs are, well, they are fucking dinosaurs. We are low on fire power and are offering you a way out. Take it or leave it," Dennis erupted, the slow boil of his impatience reaching its peak.

For a moment, nobody spoke, and the echo of Dennis's rage through the cave around them.

"Don't you think we have tried that?" Nattie spoke her own rage rising in retaliation.

"I don't know what you have tried, but it hasn't gotten you very far," Dennis spat.

"Hey, Dennis, take it easy, man," Clarke began.

"Fuck no, dude. You can be all calm and fucking zen, but look at where we are. You remember that time in the Congo? Fucking hell. What about the Sudan? That was a real liquid-shit storm. I'd call that a cakewalk compared to this. I don't care what they think, or what they have been through, they need to come with us, because I sure as holy fuck ain't gonna sit here playing pissing Jumanji for the rest of my life."

Dennis was panting by the time he finished, his rage a white-knuckled, all-encompassing experience, and yet, Clarke could not help but be impressed with how well he managed to restrain himself.

"We cannot leave yet," Nattie answered, the air of snootiness slapped from her mouth by the foul-tempered tirade she just witnessed.

"Why the fuck not?" Dennis snapped his answer almost before Nattie had finished talking.

"Because ... because we have someone here who is injured, and we cannot move him. We lost a lot to reach this place, and ... well, I can't leave him." She held the grief back from her voice, but the flicking light of the fire made her tear-filled eyes sparkle.

"Show us," Clarke walked forward, approaching the group. The closer he got the fire, the more he saw how scared they were. Even Abbott, who Clarke knew could handle himself, had the look of a boy staring down an offensive line several years older than himself.

Nattie nodded and people moved to one side. The man lay behind them, shivering and silent. His sweat-soaked body lit up in the flames as if encrusted with diamonds. His skin was pale, bordering on translucent in places. The veins looking almost black as they traced their way over his body. He only had one leg. The bloodied stump of the other had been bandaged with shirts. Even from distance, Clarke could smell the rot eating away at it.

"He's one of ours," Clarke said in an off-handed comment.

"Yes, he was a guard, and ... and my—"

"You don't have to say it," Clarke replied, placing a hand on Nattie's shoulder.

"He's going to die. I know it, we all do, but ... he's not woken up since we got here, and I don't want him to die alone. What if he comes around before it's over? He will think we abandoned him." Nattie kept from crying, keeping her voice low in order to maintain a modicum of control.

"I understand. I've got some medic training skills, let me take a look. Why don't you stand back for a second? No need for you to see it." Clarke softened his demeanour, adjusting from military to mixed social company with ease.

Nattie stepped away, back into the group, where Rob and his girlfriend took her into their arms.

Clarke crouched down and gingerly removed the dressing. He stopped himself from gagging at the chocking odour of decay, which grew stronger with every layer of bandage he removed. The limb had been torn away, rather than removed with any degree of skill. The jagged flesh had ripped in all directions, the meat and nerves left behind, dangling like tentacles. The skin around the stump was hot with infection, red and inflamed all the way to the man's crotch. Even in the dim, flicking light offered by the fire, the extent of the man's injuries was horrifically clear.

The flesh hard turned black from the outside in, like mincemeat left out for too long. Flies buzzed around his head, and in the centre of the meat, clinging to the bone as they spread outwards, writhing maggots feasted on the decaying flesh.

The man gave a groan, but for the rest, he remained oblivious to his plight.

Clarke lowered the leg, pulled a medi-pack out of his pack and quickly cleaned the wound as best he could, and re-wrapped it.

The entire process was merely for show. The man would not survive more than a day or so.

"He's in bad shape, I'm not going to lie to you. He's hurting bad. The leg is infected." Clarke looked at Nattie, who stared back at him. She needed to hear this. "He will be lucky to survive the night. If he does, then he won't make it through tomorrow."

"Is he in pain?" Nattie asked, the tremor in her voice stronger now.

"I don't know, but if he can feel anything, then yes." Clarke walked over to Nattie, and took her hands in his. "I can help."

The three words hung in the air, their meaning not lost on anybody.

"How?"

"We have a drug with us, a form of morphine. I can give it to him. He wouldn't feel a thing, and he would be at peace." Clarke looked Nattie in the eyes, searching her.

"Do it," she said, fighting back the tears.

The silence in the cave became stifling as everybody watched, afraid to cry or make any sound as Clarke took both his and Dennis's morphine-based solution and injected them into Nick Cage's arm.

His breathing quickened, and his body went momentarily stiff before he relaxed. His breathing steadied, and after a few moments, his chest fell still.

His passing seemed to trigger a cool chill, which swept through the cave.

On the fire, a piece of wood burst with a sharp crack. Several people jumped, unable to silence their surprised gasps.

"We need to get moving. The daylight won't last forever," Dennis said, his voice strictly business.

"Go, go where?" Caroline asked.

"Yes, do tell, I am just dying to relocate … oh wait, no I'm not," the whiny French voice spoke up again.

"We need to move to the third island. There is an underground communications room. We can sit tight and radio for help," Dennis said, reiterating what Clarke had already explained.

"We are here on some secret base nobody knows exists. Do you really think that anybody will come looking for, or even find us?" Nattie spoke, her voice emotionless as she continued to process Nick's passing.

"Not just anybody, but there is a direct line through to the Black Arrow control room, which you can be sure also connects to whichever government agency you all swore secrecy to. Those bastards insisted on it," Clarke said. "We just need to get there. Now tell us about this place. What have you seen, heard? I want to know everything."

The group moved to the other wing of the cave. Even in harsh times, the basics of modern civilisation prevailed. The group had split the cave into a social and a sleeping area.

The social area revealed the extent of their supplies. Boxes of meal replacements and protein bars were stacked against one wall, and a small arsenal of weapons stood against the other, hidden in the peripheries of visibility by the firelight.

"We made two trips back to the compound to get food and weapons, but we lost some of the ammo when they attacked us." Christopher Abbott showed the two men the armoury he had created. Four M16s, six pistols, and enough ammunition to take down a few dinosaurs before they had to fall back on Dennis and his blades.

"It's not much, but it will do," Clarke said, crouching down to check each weapon.

"What things?" Dennis asked. "You mean the dinosaurs?"

"He means the pygmies," Rob answered. He stood by the fire with Caroline pressed close against him.

"Pygmies? This island has fucking pygmies now?" Dennis spat, holding back an exasperated laugh. "Just fucking great."

"How dangerous are they?" Clarke asked, rising back to his feet.

"They are vicious. Small and fast, you couldn't shoot them if you tried. They'd rip you apart quicker than any dinosaur I've ever seen. Their teeth are like daggers, and they don't seem to feel pain," Rob replied.

"Ugh, must we talk about those hideous creatures?" Remi continued to whine.

"Yeah, it's true. I kicked one right in the nuts, and it just tried to eat my foot," Caroline chipped in.

"Great, so how many are there?" Dennis asked.

"Impossible to tell. They move so fast. They are smart, or at least when it comes to hunting. They attack in packs, in and out as quick as you can see them, but you know there are more, just waiting in the shadows."

"What about the dinosaurs?" Clarke asked, pushing a fresh clip into his M16.

"There's plenty of them. I'm no expert, but you've got raptors and triceratops down in the woods. They are the angry ones at least. There are lots of smaller things that I haven't ever seen before, in books or what-have-you," Abbott replied, moving back towards the fire.

"What about up here?" Dennis picked up on the next question Clarke planned to ask.

"Up here, you have various forms of ... I don't know, rex, or something. No T-rexes. We've not seen them yet, but other ones that look like 'em. Also, those things with domed heads, and ones with a single horn, like a dinosaur-unicorn. Fucking weird to look at, but they will charge anything they see." Rob took his turn to answer.

"Sounds like fun," Clarke said. He was a constant source of motion, preparing to move at a moment's notice. If not checking the weapons or his pack, he was adjusting the same, making sure he was ready.

"How far is it to the other island?" Nattie asked.

"Well, I wanted to use the walkway, but that plan has gone up in smoke. Quite literally," Clarke answered her, as he started to hand out weapons. "We will need to trek to the coast, and find a way to cross the inlet. From there, we should be able to take the ATVs and move up to the security building."

"Oh is that all? Why don't we stop along the way for a swim and maybe some sunbathing, I need to top up on my tan," Henri chimed in.

Clarke growled, his body stiff with anger. "Is he always like that?"

"You get used to Henri after a while," Nattie answered. "He grows on you."

"Yeah, like a fucking fungus," Dennis muttered under his breath.

"I heard that," Henri said, his voice forcefully dropping in pitch to make himself sound sterner.

"Yeah, well, suck it up, buttercup, we are moving out," Dennis snarled.

"My impatient friend is right. Here, take a gun and get in line," Clarke said, handing a rifle to Rob and Caroline. Abbott took one, grimacing as he slung it over shoulder. Clarke kept the final one as a spare. Caroline took a Glock, as did Nattie, who slid it into her waistband like a pro.

Henri took one under protest. Dennis grabbed one, while Clarke and Abbott took the last two.

"I don't know what to do with this," Henri complained.

"Good, just hold it until someone else runs out," Dennis called back down the line.

Dennis led the group out of the cave, with Rob behind him offering directions on how to get back down to the floor. Caroline and Henri were in the middle, with Nattie moving just before Clarke. The single file was necessary for passage over the cliffs, across the branch, and down the knotted vine ladder.

"Which way?" Rob asked, looking around the group.

They had broken formation, with the three military men forming a shield around the scientists. Nattie also stood watching the trees.

"Let's move together. We stop for nothing. If we keep moving and nothing gets in our way, we should be at the security compound before sundown," Clarke spoke.

Nobody had anything else to say, and so they set off, deeper into the jungle.

CHAPTER 21

Johan and Sikke worked their way through the bottle of whiskey before they started exchanging stories of their youth.

Johan was surprised at the hard life the director had endured. The son of Dutch immigrants, he witnessed both his mother murdered by a home intruder when he was just seven, and his father during an evening walk through a Chicago park when he was sixteen.

His career had been a series of successes, which Johan both knew and recognized as being borne from the grit embedded in the man's soul by his childhood.

Johan talked about his life growing up in post-war Austria. His father died supporting the Führer. He and his mother fled through the Netherlands and Belgium into France, and later, England. After finishing his studies, he fell into the seedy side of the London business district, and from there, history was written. His double life saw companies built and sold, while an empire was created and dominated in the dark. Wives and three children followed, but none stayed. Johan spoke to his kids and loved them dearly. All were set for life, but none knew of his business dealings. He did not want to bring them into that part of his life.

As the sun rose, and the storm quietened, they returned to talking business.

Sikke made the necessary calls, and after several lengthy phone calls, several of which Johan was not privileged enough to listen to, the decision was made, and the troops were assembled.

"We have a carrier strike group in the vicinity of the islands. They are going to divert a destroyer to the islands to rescue our people," Sikke said as he walked back into the library.

"You just happen to have a strike group close to the islands," Johan replied before he had the chance to control his tone.

"Yes, only a routine patrol. To be honest, it is more of a half group, but they were close by and, well, there was no time to lose." Sikke typed into his phone as he spoke.

"Do you really expect to find them alive?" A familiar feeling of distrust gnawed at Johan's gut. In all of his years, several business associates had tried to double cross him. None had lived long enough to regret it.

Even though Johan and Sikke were alone, and had many years of quiet dealings, the guise of a friendly visit was a thinly-veiled mask. Johan regretted sending Godfrey to the island, but he needed his eyes and ears on the ground, especially with Clarke and Amare together.

"It is not just about finding them alive, but about recovering what was being worked on. I am sure you of all people, Johan, understand the value of data. If the island is lost, then we will clean it out and ensure that when it is re-discovered, nobody will be any the wiser as to what was going on over there.

"What is going on?" Johan asked.

Sikke looked at him, his face expressionless, but for a brief second, something flashed behind his eyes. It was gone quicker than a shadow passing overhead in a stiff autumn breeze, but Johan caught it. "We went over this last night. I think that whiskey is getting to you, my friend. We were experimenting with dinosaur DNA, looking for any lost secrets."

Johan knew Sikke was lying, but there was little he could do. He would need to play it slow, wait for his moment.

"Do you play snooker, Director?" Johan asked.

"I don't believe I have ever had the opportunity," Sikke replied, the veil of friendship replaced, thinner and dirtier than before.

"Then I insist, you must learn. Tell me, how long will it be before this breakaway group reach the islands," Johan stressed his question in all the right places.

Sikke's confident step hitched. He stopped and smiled at Johan. "If all goes to plan, they should already be there."

CHAPTER 22

Captain Simon Kincaid stood on the bridge of the *USS Langley* and studied the flat seas. The first of the three islands was close. They could make out the beaches and the fortified defences. Camera imagery was enlarged and manipulated by the techs borrowed from the *USS Eisenhower* showed the damage that had been reported by the satellites.

For the rest, the island seemed secure, but he knew there could be no chances taken. The first island was to be secured, at all costs. That section of the briefing had even been underlined in triplicate before the message was sent.

"Hot Pocket One is within range, sir," Kincaid's XO, Lieutenant Howard Lloyd, spoke. "All sensors are coming back clear, and early detection readings have no signals coming back from the men stationed there, sir."

"Thank you, Mr. Lloyd. Ready one of the choppers," Kincaid said, his eyes focused on the island.

The information they had been given was limited to that which they needed to know. Kincaid had been around long enough to know that was how it worked. He had completed missions with less intel, and under worse conditions. With his eyes firmly set on reaching the rank of major in the near future, he could ill-afford to start asking too many questions now.

"Tell Gunnery Sergeant Plummer to report to the bridge," he added after a moment's thought.

Five minutes later, a burly marine entered the bridge and stood before the CO. He stood sharply to attention, his eyes focused forward, not taking in anybody in particular, but not missing anything either.

"Thank you for joining us, Gunnery Sergeant." Kincaid was a fair man, and while he ran a tight ship, he made sure that his crew knew their best efforts were appreciated. "I have a job for you. Take three marines and a chopper. Do a quick recon route above the island. Land if there is space and take a look. We need to make sure that whatever is in the main building is still locked away and secure."

"Yes, sir, is there anything else, sir?" Plummer's deep, gravelled voice had a loud and resonating quality to it.

"Yes, there is one more thing. We are under direct orders not to enter the building. We are to ensure it is secure, clear out any unfriendlies we may find, and high-tail it back out to this boat. Am I clear? I don't want any gung-ho, hero bullshit going on. No matter what happens." While fair, everybody on board knew better than to even flirt with the line. Orders were given, and orders were followed. Taking liberties were not acceptable, nor were they tolerated.

"Yes, sir. We will be ready for the off in ten minutes." Gunnery Sergeant Plummer turned, and left the bridge.

"Reduce our speed. Let the chopper make a loop around before we swing out and move for the rear island," Captain Kincaid ordered as he walked, pacing back to his captain's spot. "Lieutenant, hail the *Anderson*. I want them to sweep closer to the shore. Patch Captain Defour through to my ready room."

"Aye, sir," The XO answered. Much like any good XO, he had anticipated the captain's request, and opened the communication lines direct from the captain's ready room.

"You have the bridge until my return, Lieutenant. Hold our course and await further advice once the chopper makes land," Kincaid called as he walked from the bridge and down to the captain's ready room.

Captain Defour of the *USS Anderson*, a nuclear-class submarine, was already on the line waiting.

"Good morning, Captain. Sorry for the interruption. We are sending a bird up to check on the first island. Once down, we will swing out to sea and come back for the third island. I want you to move in closer to the shore, and keep an eye out for anything that may be displeased with our arrival." Captain Kincaid was on the wrong side of fifty, but commanded a great deal of respect from his peers.

"Yes, sir. Do you really believe it?" the young submarine captain asked.

"Do you really think the military would lie to us, Captain?" Kincaid's voice was stern.

"No, no, sir, but well … I mean, you read the orders, it does seem a little, far-fetched," the submarine captain stuttered.

"Captain Defour, we are the nation that put a man on the moon. We created nuclear weapons, and later this year will be launching a manned space flight to Mars. Reading that briefing merely made me think about the wonders we have achieved and possibilities that lie ahead." Kincaid was playing for promotion. He knew that anybody could be listening to them at any time.

The truth was, he found the entire operation absurd, but that did not mean it was a lie. He would keep an open mind, and that meant being prepared for anything. If it meant dinosaurs, then so be it.

"I understand, Captain Kincaid," Defour answered, his voice was that of a man who had been reprimanded and knew he had been wrong.

"Very good. Stick close to the coast. I want you ready with those MK-45's as soon as one of those things displays the slightest bit of aggression." Kincaid ended the communication and look at himself in the mirror.

His greying hair had, at one point in time, been jet black. Now he looked more like a salt-and-pepper combo. *Perfectly seasoned.* Splashing his face with cold water, he straightened his uniform and headed back to the bridge.

CHAPTER 23

"How much longer is it going to be?" Remi whined as they made their way through the trees.

He had not stopped complaining since they left, using every available moment to voice is annoyances.

"Will you shut the royal fuck up?" Dennis shot back at him, spinning around to face the annoying Frenchmen.

"I'm sorry, but these shoes were not made for this sort of trekking. I mean, it is bad enough I had to wear them in the lab all day long, but out here, in the mud and the—"

"Thank Christ, he learned to keep his mouth shut," Dennis said at the sudden silence.

A few moments later, Caroline screamed. The two Black Arrow men spun around, their rifles raised.

Remi lay on the floor, a pool of thick blood spreading around him. His body twitched, the bloody stump of his neck projected thick gushes of crimson into the forest.

Behind him stood a three-meter-tall beast with a head the size of a coffee table. Blood dribbled from the giant mouth as it swallowed Remi's head in a single gulp.

For a second, everybody froze. The dinosaur stood still, watching the others, and likewise, they stood staring at it.

The creature growled, a deep, guttural sound that seemed to blast from within its chest, emanating like a music from a loudspeaker.

"Get down," Christopher called.

Rob grabbed Caroline and pulled her out of the way just as Christopher opened fire.

He sprayed round after round into the creature, who turned and made to charge them down.

Dennis and Nattie joined in the fire fight, ploughing round after round into the beast until blood leaded from its flank like water through a colander.

The creature stood still, breathing heavy, wet inhalations. Gargling as it drowned in its own blood, the smaller version of the

Tyrannosaurus rex shuddered and collapsed, its legs giving way beneath it.

The beast fell atop Remi's body, which exploded in a shower of entrails and gore.

"Keep moving; we need to get to the coast," Abbott ordered, gesticulating for everybody to follow him.

Dennis took point and moved off at a pace, putting a little distance between himself and the rest. This way, he could give a warning of any danger, not to mention clear a path for them to push through.

The forest was clear, and they made a hurried retreat to the coast. Clarke led the way. Having been on the island before, he had an understanding for how they had set things up. Precaution under any circumstance, that was something he learned in his youth, and it was a motto he continued to live by. He always learned the best ways to escape, so that should the shit ever hit the fan, he would know where to head.

The forest ended in a rocky cliff that dropped twenty feet down to a stone beach. The tide was high, which worked in their favour.

"Look down there. There is a small cave that we converted into a storage house. There are two small craft in there that can take us across the water to the rear island," Clarke said, pointing to the beach.

"That's great, it really is," Rob answered. "But how in the heck are we supposed to get down there?"

"We climb, genius," Dennis growled, his attitude growing more fowl by the minute. He walked along the cliff, leaning over at regular intervals, looking for a way down. "Here, this is the easiest spot."

Without waiting, he crouched down, turned around, and swung his legs over the edge.

Dennis made short work of the descent, scampering down the rocks like they were his own backyard.

"How are we supposed to—" Caroline began, but her words cut off when the trees behind them twitched and branches started to snap.

"Learn fast. Trust me, it's easier than it looks," Clarke said, trying to sound patient as he helped Caroline swing her body over the edge.

One by one, everybody started the climb. Clarke was soon on the ground beside Dennis, with Rob a surprising second.

"That wasn't too bad," he said, breathing heavily.

Caroline joined them along with Nattie, the two females making light work of the rocky descent. They brushed their hands against their clothes, wiping away the slime that had collected on the middle portion of the cliff.

The group stood waiting, staring up the cliff. Abbott struggled to make much progress, his useless arm impeding his ability to climb at any rate.

"Jesus, he's not going to make it," Clarke said under his breath.

Dennis raised the rifle and looked through the sights. Nattie was about to say something when he pulled the trigger.

The burst of fire hit the inquisitive dinosaur and caved in the left hand side of its head. The body collapsed against the edge of the cliff, blood and brain matter dribbling down the rocks.

Abbott made it half way down the cliff before he stopped. He turned his head and looked down at the group waiting for him.

His face was drenched with sweat, and the pain coursing through his body threatened to push him into unconsciousness. He tried to move again, easing himself down the rocks, but they had become slippery, and his grip was not strong enough. He fell backwards, and landed on the stony beach with a heavy thud.

Nattie screamed, catching her voice before it rose too loud. The group ran towards Abbott; whose broken body lay with limbs pointing at all angles apart from the natural ones.

Caroline took one look at the mangled body and turned to vomit.

"I'm sorry, Zippy," Clarke said, crouching down to his colleague.

Abbott turned his eyes to look at the group. They were all he could still move. His body felt numb. He could smell his own blood surrounding him, and in the periphery of his vision, he saw the crimson flood spread.

He blinked a few time, and tears blurred his fading vision.

"We need to move, now," Dennis said, his voice filled with urgency.

"We can't just leave him," Caroline cried, her words forced through the tears.

"I don't think we have much choice in the matter," Clarke spoke, confirming what Dennis said.

The group turned and saw three large lizard-like creatures making their way down the beach. Each one looked as large as a car, their long snouts a cross between the mouth of a crocodile and an elephant's trunk.

They spied the group and gave a snarling roar.

"We need to move," Clarke said, placing is hands on Nattie's shoulders to turn her away. As the group's leader, he knew they would follow her lead sooner than his own.

"I'm sorry, Zipster," Rob whispered, his eyes brimming with tears. He stayed crouched down with his new friend for as long as he could.

"Rob, come on." Caroline cried.

"There's nothing you can do, mate," Clarke added, urging Rob to move.

Turning, Rob sprinted after the others who were making their way along the beach toward the storage cave. He didn't turn around, even when he heard the wet tearing sound of the lizards ripping his friend apart. He was just glad that Abbott couldn't scream, because he did not think he could have carried on otherwise.

The boats looked like a cross between a jet ski and a life boat. It looked as if some mad engineer had experimented, cutting and welding the two together just because he could.

Still, they floated on the water and could accommodate everybody that was left. The beach had emptied, and the lizards had disappeared, as too had Abbott's body.

They tried not to think about it.

Caroline, Rob, and Clarke took one boat-ski, and Dennis carried Nattie on the other. Nattie and Rob stood with rifles at the ready. The all knew the firepower would be useless against anything that may attack from them the water, but they found solace in knowing they would go down swinging.

The craft moved fast, bouncing over the waves, bringing them ever closer to the rear island and the salvation that lay in wait.

CHAPTER 24

The SeaHawk rose from the deck of the *Langley* and immediately banked to the left, moving to pass over the first island in a clockwise motion. Sergeant William How sat behind the controls. An experienced pilot, he had seen action all over the world and was one of the biggest sceptics in the Navy.

"That's some thick jungle down there," How's voice cracked through the headsets.

"Don't worry about the jungle. It's the compound we need to secure," Gunnery Sergeant Plummer spoke, his gruff voice as serious as a winter blizzard. "Remember, ladies, we can look but not touch. Just imagine I'm your old lady and we are walking down the promenade in the middle of summer."

"Heck Gunney, if a piece of ass is fine enough, my old lady would understand," Sergeant Elroy Woods said with a laugh.

"Well, I know what you consider a fine piece of ass, Woods, and as long as you check she has a clean health certificate, then rock on, my son," Plummer answered, much to the amusement of all but Woods.

"We don't know what has happened, but all we need to do is check that the structure here is intact and all is well, then we get back to the boat," Plummer said, reiterating their orders.

Each man nodded in turn as their CO's eyes fell on them.

"Woods, I want you and Langston to take the jungle side, scan the trees, and make sure there isn't anything nasty lying in wait. I will check the perimeter of the building. How, I want you to stay with the chopper. This is a quick in and out, and you will be well positioned to lay down covering fire if needed by either of us."

"Aye, sir," the voices sounded.

"For the love of God, what was that?" How's startled voice came through their headsets like an alarm.

The chopper lurched to the left for a moment before the experienced marine brought it back under control.

"Everything alright up there?" Plummer asked, concerned.

"Aye, sir. All good. I thought I saw something, but … but I couldn't have." It was clear that Plummer didn't believe his answer.

"If we have hostiles down there, we need to be sure. Take us around for another circuit," Plummer ordered, sliding open the chopper's side door.

The SeaHawk made a tight turn, and for a moment, all anybody saw were trees. Then they saw it, they all saw it, but none could believe their eyes. Nobody spoke for fear of being wrong and deemed insane.

"Sergeant How, set this bird on the ground," Plummer ordered, before turning to look at his men. "Change of plan. We stick together. We need to find out what the heck is going on down here. Watch your step, and hold your fire until we know what is going on."

The helo spun around in a tight circle as it tried to settle on the patch of cleared ground between the tree line and the compound.

The marines were out and gathered in an arrowhead formation before the full weight of the bird had touched down.

"Move towards the compound. Langston, Woods, keep your eyes on the trees," Plummer instructed as the group set off.

They made short work at reaching the compound. Experienced men, tough men, who, between them, had seen blood-shed across the four corners of the globe, were reduced to jumping at shadows on the small island.

"The main entrance looks clear. Let's run a perimeter check, and then report back to the boat. Something is going on around here, and I don't like it." Plummer gave the orders. Not one to admit fear, raising a point of concern for the safety of his men was a different matter.

"Aye, Gunny. Shall we split up?" Sergeant Langston asked, the quiver in his voice an audible plea for a negative.

"Negative, Sergeant. We stick together. Keep your eyes peeled on the jungle." There was no play or jest in the words. It was serious business; behind enemy lines, with an army closing down on you, serious.

"Sergeant How, do you copy?" Plummer called back to the helo as they disappeared from view behind the rear of the square built building.

"Yes, sir, Gunnery Sergeant. I'm here, and I have some company, so don't you worry. Take your time," Sergeant How replied, his voice wonder-filled, almost childlike in its tone.

Something about the words haunted Plummer, who took a step back and stared up at the two story building.

Aside from some minor storm damage, there was nothing to point at there being anything wrong in the compound. It didn't make any sense.

Behind them, in the trees, a branch crunched, a loud, crisp sound which saw them all spin around, weapons raised.

"There is something out there, Gunny," Langston whispered as he slowly brought his rifle up to his shoulder.

"Stand down, soldier. We didn't come here to start no fights. If they come, we will sure as fuck end it, but start something? Nope. This is not our problem," Plummer ordered but could not pull his eyes away from the trees.

Whatever stood there was big. They could all see it, but just not with enough clarity to believe their eyes. A shadow inside a shadow was no sign for an all-out assault.

Plummer looked back at the building. Somehow, the concrete structure had changed. It now loomed over them, the windows dark gashes in its flank. From that perspective, it looked more like a prison. He knew why. Keeping people in was not the idea behind its construction, but rather, keeping that native wildlife out.

The trio moved around the back of the building and made their way back along the long second side. The trees were closer here, the cleared area now wider than a house.

"Hold your step," Plummer called, stopping suddenly, flinging his arms out wide.

"Holy hell, would you look at that," Woods said, crouching down to study the thin wire that snaked its way along the trees. "If that thing watching us—"

"We will be blown to bits," Plummer finished, his eyes following the fine silver wire as it moved through the crudely fashioned minefield. "If they haven't set it off yet, then we should be good to go. Just take it slow, people, nobody get any funny ideas."

As he moved, Gunnery Sergeant Plummer released his rifle, letting it fall on its strap. The others followed suit, and the three men snuck their way along the building.

They saw the helicopter, saw Sergeant How standing with his back to them, his hands at his sides, oblivious to their presence. His attention was focused away from them, and a few strides later, as they came fully clear of the building, they saw it also. Their stride faltered, and the three marines came to a halt beside one another.

"Jesus wept," Plummer growled.

The dinosaur was enormous, at least twenty feet long from nose to tip; a few extra inches if you included the length of the four curled spikes the extended from its tale. The beast stood twice as tall as any man, taller at the hump of its shoulders, and taller still when the large pentagonal plates that rose from its back like fins were taken into account.

The dark green body blended into the colours of the forest, while the large plates that lined the length of its body, from the tip of the tail to the curve of its snout, moved from the same dark green to a deep red colour.

The beast walked, moving out of the trees as it crossed the rear of the exposed compound before disappearing into the trees again to be swallowed by the darkness the second it passed into the forest.

The sound of its heavy footsteps was nothing to the swish of the vertical plates, which seemed to flow independently as it moved. The long tail swung back and forth, crashing into the trunk of a tree, tearing deep gouges in the bark.

"What the hell was that?" Langston asked.

"That was … that … that … was a stegosaurus," Woods answered, shocked.

"No shit, Sherlock. You didn't need to answer him," Plummer snarled, eager to regain a sense of normalcy. He found it in his standard, charming disposition.

"I guess we know what was following us," Woods said timidly.

"Wait, you think another one—" Langston stopped talking as the second creature moved into view, following an identical route as its larger, slightly more impressive brother.

"They are patrolling," Plummer said as the three men walked up to the waiting helo.

Sergeant How turned to meet them. "I don't know what's going on here, Gunny, but they don't seem to mind us being here. It's like they just plain ignored us."

"There is something off about this entire island, Sergeant. Let's get airborne," Plummer ordered, not stopping to admire the view any longer than necessary. A third hulking beast, the largest so far, appeared. Its lumbering gait saw its body sway from side to side as it moved, with the man-sized plates on its back moving at a delay, meaning they swung in the opposite direction to the body most steps.

Plummer squinted, his sharp eyes catching sight of something as the creature moved passed them. "Well, I'll be fucked," he said, offering no more on the subject.

With the four men on board, Sergeant How took them into the air and out to sea, but not before making one final spin around. With their eyes and minds adjusted, they could pick out the trail of the three stegosauruses as they wandered through the trees. Their path was slowly being beaten into the ground, a worn out circle just beyond the perimeter of the island's compound.

"That was odd," Langston said, sitting back as the land beneath their feet gave way to the ocean.

"Yeah, and I have a feeling it is only going to get weirder," Plummer answered, his eyes focused on the destroyer ahead of them.

CHAPTER 25

The inlet was calm, which made their trip across to the third island an uneventful one. Yet, that did not stop them from standing frozen on the shore filled with apprehension.

While none had chosen to mention it for fear of spreading panic, the solid ground beneath the feet loosened their tongues. Both Nattie and Caroline had been sure of a shadow circling beneath their craft as they made the crossing. Rob was also sure he had seen something, although he maintained it could easily have been a simple trick of the waves.

"There was something out there. I've seen it before," Clarke said, not bothering to cushion his words. "Big bastard too."

"Why didn't you warn us?" Caroline asked, shocked.

"If I told you, you would have worried about it. We needed to get across. We didn't have another option, so it seemed pointless information under the circumstances." Clarke flashed her a smile as he spoke. It was a look which, coupled with his ruggedly handsome features, had melted the heart of many a slapper in the bars up and down the mainland US. Caroline, however, appeared to be immune to his charms.

"You're an asshole," she spat, eliciting a deep chuckle from Dennis.

"She's got your number, mate," he said, stressing the final word with a thick Australian lilt.

"Yeah, well, I'll live, and thanks to us, so will all of you. Now pull your knickers out of your butt crack and let's get moving." Clarke's sunken mood told everybody enough, and they followed his movements without question.

The first building stood in remarkably good condition, until you reached the hall that lead to the walkway that connected the islands.

They did not check for survivors. Clarke pointed out not long after they started moving that if anybody saw them, they would either call for help, or open fire. He did not seem to give any indication to his preference, but he moved with the gait of a man itching for a fight.

The quads were located around the back of the building, an area cast in deep shadow.

"There are three bikes, so we will need to tandem up," Clarke instructed. "Dennis, you ride ahead, I'll take the doc here. Lovebirds, I want you to ride in the middle. Keep your eyes open."

Once again, nobody dared argue with the man, whose face looked like looming thunder.

Dennis set off first, speeding down the muddy track, not caring whether the others followed or not.

"I'll drive, you man the guns," Caroline said to Rob, throwing her leg over the quad as she settled in behind the handlebars. "What?"

"Can you handle on of those things, missy?" Clarke asked, stunned.

"Bitch, please. I grew up on a farm, I've been riding quads since before I was a teenager. Besides, Rob is a better shot than me, so it makes sense." The pair were off almost before Rob was seated on the vehicle.

They disappeared into the trees and were gone, the sound of their engine beat an aggressive tune on the quiet island.

"I guess that just leaves us, mate," Nattie said with a smile.

"Knock it off, would ya? Bad enough I have to put up with that shit from Dennis," Clarke grumbled.

"Sure thing. You cheer up a little, and I'll knock off the whole Australian thing," Nattie negotiated.

"Cheer up? You do know where we are, right?" Clarke looked at her, unsure as to why she felt any need for cheer.

"Yes, I know where we are. I also know we are alive. We have survived, and that in itself is reason for cheer. Besides, I don't want to die with some grumpy old man beside me." Nattie slid a new magazine into the rifle and sat down behind Clarke, who nodded at her and flashed a half-smile.

"That's better," Nattie answered.

"You are all fucking nuts," Clarke uttered under his breath, the words drowned out by the roar of the engine.

They drove with a small gap between them, never reducing it to less than five meters or increasing to more than ten. They were not alone. Everybody knew that, and each of them had, at different times, spotted movement through the trees.

The forest seemed denser on this island, the darkness created in places by the tall overhead canopy seeming that much darker.

The dinosaur came out of nowhere, charging through the trees like a bipedal bull. Its large domed head looked like a vision of Christ with his crown of thorns. The spiked horns ringed the base of the domed skull, which collided with Dennis before he had the chance to react.

He was sent flying from his quad, which continued driving for some way without anybody behind the controls. Dennis landed in a heap on the floor, and the dinosaur just kept on coming. Three more charged out of the trees behind it, running towards, and over, the downed Black Arrow man.

Nattie raised her gun to fire, but Clarke bellowed for her to stop. Her reactions were fast, and she released the pressure on the trigger just before it was too late.

In the middle, Rob never had the chance to take aim because Caroline spun the quad around in a donut, bringing it to a stop just as the last beast ran over the spot where Dennis lay.

Nattie and Rob were off their vehicles in no time and over beside Dennis in a sprint.

He lay still, his eyes closed. A deep wound on his scalp, just behind his hairline, painted his face with a scarlet mask.

"Dennis," Nattie called.

The man groaned in response, which in itself was a relief.

"Help me get him to us," Rob said, looking around the trees, waiting for the next attack to arrive.

"I don't think that is a good idea, mate," Clarke replied. "That leg is busted pretty bad."

Only then did they look at the Dennis and notice the way one of his legs was twisted at over a ninety-degree angle when compared to the rest of his body.

"Holy shit," Rob said. "We need to set that a little if we want to move him."

"Whatever it is, do it fast. Something spooked those things, and if they were scared, we should be too," Caroline spoke.

"They attacked us," Nattie said.

"No, trust me. I've seen enough spooked cattle and such to know fear in a beast when I see it. Something scared those things, and that means we should be terrified."

As if on cue, a roar tore through the forest that made the roots of the trees tremble, sending a vibrations of fear through the muddy ground.

"What was that?" Nattie asked, spinning around with her rifle raised.

"Something that will eat that rifle for a breakfast and us as dessert," Clarke said, understanding the need for haste.

"Move him onto the quad. Caroline, you and Rob take point; just follow the road, there's only one way. Nattie, you take the second bike and I'll come with him," Clarke spoke fast as the rumble in the trees drew closer.

Panic spread through the group. They focused their energies and between them, managed to lift Dennis onto the back of a quad. It was an uncomfortable fit, and undoubtedly bad for his leg, but they managed it. Luck was on their side when Dennis passed out, his agonised screams falling silent.

"Hurry," Clarke called to the others as the thunder of the approaching danger drowned out the revving of his quad's engine.

They set off at a pace, spinning wheels kicking up thick streams of mud just as the beast appeared. The Tyrannosaurus charged through the trees, smashing trunks and uprooting smaller examples without so much as slowing down.

Caroline screamed as she saw the beast behind them. Easily the size of two busses, its body belied belief. The long counter-balancing tail extended behind it, whipping and scything deep gouges into the flanks of the nearby trees.

The air around them vibrated as the king of beasts stood tall and surveyed the area that was its own. The speeding quads caught its eyes, for the roar that followed them was one of pure, unfiltered rage.

The ground shook as the beast gave chase, its barking howls chilling the sweat that formed on their flesh.

The quads skidded and slid their way down the muddy trail. The forest sped by in a blur. The building appeared before them. A small concrete structure, it did not look strong enough to keep them safe from a rampaging T-rex. Yet, it offered them a modicum of refuge, and they would take it.

Caroline sped towards the building, circling behind it without slowing down.

"What are you doing?" Rob asked when the quad came to a sudden and jarring halt.

"There was no storage around the front, which means it is back here. Look." Caroline pointed to the open fronted extension that grew from the rear corner of the building. "I put money on that door here being open, or at least breakable."

The other quads appeared and everything happened at such a pace that Rob had no time to question anything.

Clarke drove his quad right into the building and jumped out. In two strides, his shoulder connected with the door, and after three thrusts, it burst open.

"Everybody inside. Rob, help me with Dennis." Clarke moved fast, not stopping for a moment.

Their disappearing act behind the building bought them some time from the charging beast that pursued them, but it would not last forever.

"What about that door?" Nattie asked as the two men rushed by, awkwardly carrying the pale and sweaty Dennis between them.

"Fuck it, we are heading underground anyway," Clarke answered. "Now hurry. Keep those weapons ready. I have no idea what could be waiting inside for us. Rob, take a gun, I've got him from here."

Clarke crouched and slung the unconscious Dennis over his shoulder. The leg of Dennis's trouser was soaked in blood, and they could see the bulge around his thigh from where the bone had broken through the skin.

"Hold on, buddy," Clarke whispered to him. "Somebody take point, goddammit."

Outside, the Tyrannosaurs moved around the building, using its frame as a battering ram to try and force entry. The walls shook and the lighting flickered, yet everything remained standing.

"Where are the stairs?" Rob asked as he led the group through the building. Hardly a soldier, Clarke could not help but be impressed by the kid's guts.

Much like the building on my main island, the layout here was remarkably similar. The corridors wound around the complex, following the building's basic structure, with rooms, both single and interconnecting, linking from them.

It made it easy for Rob to lead them to the same area he knew of from the main building.

"Nattie, come on," Caroline said as they stood by the reinforced steel door on the lower level of the building.

"This is where it all began," Nattie spoke, more to herself than anybody else.

Above them, the sound of footsteps plodding through the halls echoed down in a series of thuds. A variety of small creatures had followed them inside, but other than providing a few jump moments, they showed no interest in attacking the group.

The constant impacts of the impatient Tyrannosaurs were a distant, semi-rhythmic thud as the beast continued to try and force its way inside.

"What?" Caroline said, confused.

"In the other building, this is where it all started. When we had to destroy the subjects with strain twelve, Ferry and I came to incinerate them. It was in this room that they escaped. They attacked Ferry, and I had to get away. I opened the door and that is when everything started to go to shit," Nattie continued to speak in a wispy, airy voice, almost as if she were not aware that she was talking at all.

"It wasn't your fault, Doc." Clarke stepped forward towards Nattie. "This place was doomed from the start." He placed his arms around her shoulders, and she allowed herself to be led inside.

Rob closed the door, which locked shut, sealing them inside.

"So what, we just have to stand here and wait?" Rob said, turning around to look at the small bare brick space.

"We can do, or we can go and call for help," Clarke said, resting Dennis on the floor. He had started to come to, groaning in his semi-conscious state.

Clarke moved to the far corner of the room, disappearing into the shroud. A few moments later, a light appeared on the floor as he opened up a trapdoor, revealing a second underground level.

"Everybody get down there," he instructed.

"Dennis, hey, buddy, come on, stay with me," Clarke whispered to his colleague. "I need you to work with me, mate."

Dennis grunted, and his eyes opened. For a moment, they were vague and distant, but soon found their focus and held Clarke's gaze. Raising his arm, Dennis draped it over Clarke's shoulder, and using his good leg, heaved himself off the floor.

He screamed into white-clenched lips as his broken leg moved, but Dennis pushed himself on. Clarke took almost all of his buddy's body weight, but they made it to the trapdoor.

"Almost there," Clarke said as he helped Dennis position himself above the ladder.

"I've got him," Rob's voice came from beneath them. His hands appeared and took the weight of the injured man.

Clarke hurried down the ladder, closing and locking the trapdoor from the inside.

Once there, he turned around and saw the others staring at him.

"What is this place?" Caroline asked, looking around the large space.

"Think of it is the ultimate panic room. From here, we can sustain ourselves long enough for a rescue party to come for us," Clarke said, moving away from the ladder and deeper into the bunker. "This place is divided into four units; sleeping, recreation, systems, and medical. We are perfectly safe down here, so make yourselves feel at home. Rehydrate some food if you want."

Clarke walked away from the group, following the bloody trail left by Rob and Dennis.

"This leg is bad, man," Rob said when he saw Clarke in the doorway. "It's fully compound, and I think his knee is also smashed. It's all mangled."

"Let me take a look." Clarke moved forward, but even his stern face paled at the sight of the mangled limb. "Fuck me."

"He passed out again as I moved him. Good thing too," Rob said, rooting around through the medical supplies.

"Yeah," Clarke answered. "What are you looking for?"

Rob did not answer straight away, but after a few moments stood up holding a small bottle of liquid. "This," he said.

"What is it?"

"Morphine. We are going to dose him up and hope for the best. You said it yourself, help will be on the way soon. Best we can do here is keep him comfortable."

Rob didn't wait for any authorization, but measured out the syringe and injected Dennis in a single fluid motion. "That should help," he spoke to Dennis, replacing the bottle and discarding the needle.

"Can you watch him?" Clarke asked.

"Sure, if you go get us out of this hell hole." Dennis tried a smile, but knew it failed.

Clarke hurried through the bunker and found the others still standing together, looking around like schoolchildren in a museum.

"Nothing will break if you touch it. Trust me. We are safe as houses down here," he called to them as he moved through to the systems room.

The room was not especially large, yet contained enough computer equipment to run a small country.

Firing up the consoles, Clarke studied the data. "Well sweet baby Jesus, would you look at that," he said to the room, not expecting anybody to response.

"What is it? Good news at last?" Nattie spoke, ignoring the slight twitch she saw in Clarke as her voice broke his concentration.

"Better than good. Everything is still running and calibrated. I was worried we would need to do some real work. Here, come and watch this for me while I try and make a call."

Clarke left the station he was standing behind and moved two tables further down. He picked up the phone received, and waited, pushing a few buttons every now and then.

"Good morning, sir, this is Clarke. I am afraid there has been a small problem," he said to whoever picked up on the other end of the line.

CHAPTER 26

Johan studied the director. Ever since his admission that troops were close by the island, Johan's gut had been screaming warnings to him.

The conversation had dropped, and a more serious air permeated the large room.

He kept his eyes on Sikke, not letting the man out of his sight. It was not a subtle change in character, but the director seemed equally willing to let the amicable nature of their meeting fall to the wayside.

The silence that had fallen only served for the alarm on Johan's tablet to sound even more siren-like than normal.

Both men moved across the large room, heading towards it as if there were some race afoot. Sikke backed off as he reached the table ahead of the old man, holding his hands up in mock surrender of the device.

"If you will excuse me, Director," Johan added as a snide remark.

"By all means, Mr. Krauss." Sikke backed up half a step, reclaiming it the moment Johan started talking.

"Go ahead, Mr. Hutchinson," Johan answered, trying hard to keep the relief he felt at hearing Clarke's voice out of his own. "I see. I understand."

As he spoke, Johan stared down Director Werkhoven, taunting him, daring him to speak up.

"You are in luck, my friend. The US Navy is nearby, they happened to be in the area. I am sure they will be able to pick you all up. You have three of their scientists with you, great. That will only bolster their best efforts, I am sure." The smile stretched across Johan's face could not have been controlled by even the most serious of poker players. "Oh, there won't be any waiting. I just happen to have a Director Werkhoven of the NSA sitting here with me. Director, you will be happy to assist with the collection of my men, won't you? Perfect. They will be with you shortly." Johan concluded and disconnected the call.

Sikke stood staring at him, his face set like thunder. "They are alive?"

"Yes, along with three scientists. I told you, Sikke, my old friend, the Black Arrow team I assembled were some of the best around."

"You must excuse me. I need to make a call." Sikke turned and left, striding out of the room like a man running late to the most important meeting of his life.

He returned a few moments later with a smug look plastered on his face.

"You have your wish, Johan. I have ordered Captain Kincaid of the *USS Langley* to send a crew to rescue my scientists, and your men." Sikke walked slowly, bouncing the mobile in his hands. He had more to say, but intended on milking it for as long as possible.

"What is really going on out there?" Johan asked, standing up straight to stare the director down.

Director Werkhoven stopped before the large windows of the snooker room. They looked out over the ocean. He looked at Johan and smiled.

"You know what, I'm going to be honest with you, Johan. You have earned that much after all the years we have worked together." The same shark-like smile spread over his face. "We are using the site to biologically engineer dinosaurs, cross breeding them to form the ultimate killer species. Through the use of biometric control, we are able to assume control of the creatures, overriding their basic neural functions and using them for our own purpose."

"What are you saying?" Johan pushed.

"Oh, don't be naïve, Johan, you know exactly what I am saying." Sikke seemed almost irritated with the question.

"You were already on the island." The realization hit Johan in the gut, despite the fact that the notion had been swinging around the dark corners of his mind ever since the director made the admission of following him.

"Bravo, bravo. Yes, we knew the islands were there, and have been using them as a storage ground of our boys. You see, we are not just building a few creatures to show off to the world, but rather, we are building a new way of life. Imagine it, dinosaurs roaming the wilds of every country on earth, keeping the population in check, all controlled by a central bank here in the United States." The grin that spread over the director's face changed. As he walked closer to Johan, the shadows of the sun behind him turned the grin into a twisted and sinister image.

"You cannot be serious." Johan did not know what else to say.

"I am as serious as an angry triceratops wandering through the suburbs. We have been planning this for a long time." Sikke gave a laugh.

"So the attacks, my men who died. They were your controls? Why? To test what you can do, to see if your monsters are working?" Johan felt his anger building. "I lost good men, honest men also, men with families."

"Unfortunately, I cannot claim any responsibility for those incidents. You see, our controls have been limited. After all, what experiment is done without control? No, we have the first island inhabited by dinosaurs fully embedded with our controls. The second we used as the control group. Real dinosaurs, wild and untamed. We needed to monitor behavioural patterns," Sikke explained.

"You are mad," Johan stammered.

"We are the United States of America. We are revolutionaries, leading the new world. This is not some fly-by-night operation. You stumbled onto a long running project, Mr. Krauss," Sikke spoke, stressing the words, as if they were of the upmost importance.

"What about the third island? What have you been building there?"

"Oh, that we left empty. It is a safe zone. When we need to start running human trials, that island will be the location we use to deliver and collect the test subjects. It is untouched by the years. Anything that survives there has been there since before we arrived." Sikke dismissed the third island, as if it were just an annoyance with its presence.

"What on earth made you do this? I don't understand. It makes no sense to me. What do you expect to achieve?" Johan's head started to spin as he tried to wrap his mind around the revelations he was hearing.

"Me? Oh no, this is not my doing. This goes above my head and through so many different levels that it makes me look like nothing more than a foot soldier."

Johan stood his ground, but was thrown by the sudden admission. His heart thundered in his chest, the steady pulse ringing in his ears like the beating of wings. "Then why all the games? Back in Hong Kong, the whole design and security detail. None of it makes any sense."

"Have you never heard of a scapegoat? Once our islands had been discovered, which we realized would only be a matter of time, as even our abilities and concealment can only go so far, we realized that we would need a cover story. It was not planned, so please, I don't want you to feel as if I used you specifically. It just turned out this way. You have to admit, it is all rather convenient." That smile spread across his lips again. "Now if you forgive me, I need to step out for a moment."

The director turned and left without saying another word, leaving Johan stood in his place, leaning onto the snooker table with both hands. It was a lot for his aged mind to process in one hit.

His heart grew louder and louder, and by the time Johan realized what really made the sound, it was too late. The helicopter came into view, travelling over the coast. Lights flared on their side, and a few moments later, thousands of rounds of smoking leading punctured the buildings ocean-facing façade.

The rounds tore through the walls, shattered the windows in a spray of broken glass and mortar dust.

Johan threw himself to the floor, wincing as the rainfall of glass shards cut into his flesh. Blood flowed from the multiple lacerations as the helicopter continued to pepper the building with round after round.

Johan needed to move. He knew it. Crawling on his belly, pulling his body over the glass, he dragged himself away. Pain exploded in his mind like a rising fountain as he took a round to the leg. His lower body caught fire, or so it felt. His fingers were flayed by the glass, to the point where the lacerations were so deep and so many, his fingertips splayed outwards like peeled bananas.

The onslaught came to an end, as Johan knew it would. He lay on the floor panting, covered in blood. His house was destroyed. The dark wood snooker table lay in a broken heap on the floor. The ceiling and walls sparked, spitting small bursts of electricity as the complex wiring behind them tried to function.

He heard footsteps and the sound of crunching glass. They seemed to echo all around Johan, making it impossible for him to locate Director Werkhoven. He knew it was him. It had to be.

"I am sorry it had to end this way, Johan. Don't worry, Black Arrow Security did a wonderful job on the island, and I mean it. To have survived so long out there, those two men must be something special. I will make sure they are treated well," Sikke said, standing with the toe of his shoes pushed against Johan's broken and bleeding face.

Johan was stuck, his aging body betraying him in the final moments. He only felt one thing, and that was the cold steel of Director Werkhoven's revolver resting against the back of his head. It was a strangely comforting feeling.

"Fuck you," Johan said. He heard the crack of the pistol, but his head exploded long before the echo of the gunshot finally died away.

CHAPTER 27

"Keep her close to the shoreline. I want us at full alert. Silence from all quarters," Captain Defour whispered his orders and heard them echo through the submarine, riding on the voices of the crew members distributing them for him.

The *Anderson* had broken away from the *Langley,* following Captain Kincaid's orders. He had been elected the commanding officer of their small and rather unique strike group, and Defour had no plans to disobey him.

After the conversation between the two men, it became clear to Defour that the briefing they had received had been truthful, no matter how unbelievable it sounded.

He understood his role and that whatever they saw or discovered around the islands would be paid for in some way or another. An occupational hazard, he had come to learn.

The submarine slipped beneath the surface. This close to the islands, the need for such tactics were simple to avoid being easily seen by any eyes on the islands.

"Arm the forward torpedoes. Hold fire until I give my mark," he whispered, and once again heard his command travel through the craft. Defour had every right to be nervous, and as he wiped the sweat from his brow, he looked around the crew. They all shared the same pensive expression.

Dinosaurs. Nobody had believed it until they had seen the few grainy photographs that came with the briefing.

"Captain, I have something on the sonar," Luke Owens whispered, looking up at the captain as he spoke. "I think you are going to want to see it."

Defour crossed the bridge to the sonar console and leaned down to read the screen.

"What the hell is that? It's huge." Standing up straight, he felt a surge of adrenaline rush through his body. The rest of the crew were watching the pair nervously.

"I don't know, Captain, but it is big, twice the size of us, and organic," Owens answered, struggling to keep his voice to a whisper.

"Hold our course. Keep an eye on that thing. If it turns towards us, then we will blow it out of the water." Defour clapped his sonar technician on the shoulder. "Bring up the forward video display. I want to see whatever it is out there."

A few moments later, as Defour moved to the captain chair, the main screen flickered to life and a shot of the ocean greeted them. The water was surprisingly clear. They could make out the shape of the creature in the distance, it's hulking frame unlike anything any of the crew had ever seen before.

"What the hell is that?" his young XO, Patrick Burke, said, his eyes transfixed on the screen.

The image continued to come into focus, like a wafting Polaroid, as the creature closed the distance on them. It seemed oblivious to their presence, set to pass around them on a trajectory that would bring it arcing around the islands, as if travelling in a loop.

"I have no idea, but it is magnificent," Defour said. Raised on the sea, by a single mother and renowned marine biologist, Captain Richard Defour held an affinity for the creatures of the ocean, which ran deeper than the mere appreciation of a fellow sub-aquatic life form.

The creature had a large oval-shaped body, with enormous flippers that extended from its front shoulders like exaggerated oars; fat and wide. They moved with a distinguished grace, powering the beast through the water with what looked to be minimal effort. While in the rear, short and squat leg-like appendages extended down into flipper-like feet.

"Captain, the creature is passing too close. Any closer and we won't be able to open fire."

"Stand down, we won't be firing anything today," Captain Defour said as the creature turned its long neck to stare at the submarine. The head was only small, compared to the size of the body at least.

"Sir?" his XO asked, daring to question the captain.

"I said stand down," Defour replied, raising his voice a little too loud.

"Aye, sir," Patrick replied, lowering his gaze.

"Hold our course, follow the islands. Take the inlet and loop around to meet up with the *Langley* again."

"Aye, sir," Burke repeated.

"XO, you have command," Defour said as he left the bridge.

As he made his way back to his quarters, Defour scratched at his head. He was stunned by what he had seen. The entire experience left him questioning his life for the first time. Joining the Navy had been his way of seeing the world, of removing a certain degree of financial burden from his mother. He was not a military man by birth rite or circumstance. His enlistment had not been a last resort or a boyhood dream. It was simply the right decision, at the right time. But now, how things can change in an instant.

As he moved through the sub, acknowledging those that saluted him as he passed, he felt closed in, confined. The walls were pressing down on him. The cylindrical tube that had been his home for many years no longer felt like a welcome place. There was more to the world, and he was missing out on it.

CHAPTER 28

The chopper landed on the deck of the *Anderson* and the captain was waiting for them.

"Gentlemen, welcome back. I trust everything was secure on the island," Kincaid addressed the four men.

"Yes, sir. The building is secure," Plummer answered, stressing the world building. He studied the captain's face.

"Very good," Kincaid answered. "Dump your gear and meet me in my ready room in fifteen minutes for a de-briefing," Kincaid said, turning away from the men, leaving them with their obviously burning questions.

"He knew what we were walking into," Sergeant Woods said as the group made their way from the helicopter, which was already being manoeuvred back inside the boat's hangar.

"Watch your words, Sergeant," Plummer growled under his breath.

"Sorry," Woods added.

The four men were in a fresh set of clothing and lined up outside the captain's ready room five minutes ahead of schedule. Woods bounced around with a nervous excitement. They all knew what they saw on the island, and understood that it was something above their paygrade.

The door to the room opened, and Captain Kincaid appeared. "Gentlemen, come in, come in."

The four men walked into the room and found themselves seated behind a large table; the four of them on one side, with the captain on the other. It was cramped, and it was purposefully set so.

"Gentlemen, congratulations to you all," Kincaid said, sitting back in his chair.

"Excuse me, sir, but we did nothing. The island was secure," Plummer spoke.

"Congratulations are in order, for you four are now part of a select group that has a certain level of knowledge that is both powerful and dangerous. As a result, as of today, your lives are going to change. Once we return from this trip, you will be relocated from your current regiments. I cannot give you any more information at this time, but I assure you, you will find the financial gains of your new positions to be very agreeable." Captain Kincaid looked at the men before him. He looked them in the eyes, and held their gaze long enough for them to understand his words were genuine, but also, that there was something else to come still.

"What do you need us to do first, sir?" Plummer asked, leaning forward, speaking for the group.

"I am glad you asked. I have just gotten off the phone with … well, let's just say they were very important people. I need to you return to the island, the third island, and retrieve some scientists that have managed to hide away in the security building." Kincaid pulled a file from beneath the table and slid it across to the men. "This is not a simple mission. There are bigger things at stake here. It is imperative that you understand this."

"Sir, you cannot be serious," Sergeant How spoke up.

"Are you questioning the orders of your commanding officer, Sergeant?" Kincaid asked, his voice stern.

"No sir, I was just seeking clarification," How answered snidely. He stared at the file, and took his turn to flip through the photographs as they were slid his way.

"Very good, I want this to be underway in ten minutes. We don't know much about the island, but intel from back home says it is clean. It is just a walk in, walk out, kind of job." Kincaid brought up the same satellite image of the island on his beamer that was in the paper file the men held. "Plummer, I want you to take one guy and head into this bay here. It will be a quick walk through the trees to the building. They will be underground in the shelter. You may need to get creative when extracting them. Bring the scientists back here, and we can all ride back to the carrier group and head on home."

"Sir, why us?" Sergeant Woods asked. He sat studying his captain's face, certain that there was more to it all that they were being told.

"Well, Sergeant, I like to think of it as you being in the right place at the right time," Kincaid said with a smile. "You are dismissed, gentlemen. Good luck out there."

Captain Kincaid remained seated, his attention moved from the men sat across from him, to the paperwork before him. On most ships, the XO took control of the administrative tasks, but Kincaid liked to keep his hands on the paper-trail grindstone when time permitted. It also served as a great tactic to get the message across to his men that their presence was no longer required.

The four men stood and left the room, none of them speaking until they were two floors down in the mess area. "Sergeant Woods, you are coming with me. Langston, stay here on the boat. The two of us can handle this. Besides, if it goes to shit, I want you in the back of the chopper laying down covering fire for us," Plummer said, giving the orders, and the men nodded their agreement.

Ten minutes later, with the final hurried bite of lunch still being chewed, Plummer and Woods were in the zodiac heading towards the shoreline.

CHAPTER 29

Clarke ended the call with Johan and sat staring at the receiver. Something was not right. He looked up and saw the others had gathered around him. Their faces were grave with concern.

"Good news," he said, trying to make it sound believable. "The marines are coming to rescue us."

"That's good, right? They can take care of the dinosaurs and stuff. I mean, they are marines," Caroline babbled, looking from Nattie to Rob, wondering why they were not cheering.

"What are you not telling us?" Rob asked, studying Clarke's pensive face.

"I don't know, but something doesn't feel right," the Australian answered.

"Something is not normally anything good," Nattie followed up.

"That was my boss, at Black Arrow. He just happened to have to have the director of the NSA in his house at the time I called. I know you don't know my boss, but he is not the kind of guy the NSA just pay a friendly visit on." Clarke didn't look at the scientists as he spoke, but rather stared at a space on the floor between them all.

It was not a particularly attractive piece of flooring, but it held his gaze while his mind spun through the different fragment of ideas and notions that bubbled within it.

"What do you think it means?" Rob asked.

"Like the doc suggested, nothing good." Clarke stood up and moved across the room, weaving through the computer terminals. He swung his rifle over his shoulders and opened fire on the wall.

The rattling thunder of the automatic fire echoed around the acoustically sound bunker like fireworks at New Year, deafening the gathered crowd.

Caroline screamed, and the others flinched, expecting bullets to go ricocheting around the room like a Saturday morning cartoon, but instead, the wall splintered and shattered. The camouflaged glass disappeared, revealing a secret armoury.

"How did you know that was there?" Caroline asked.

"Lucky guess," Clarke answered, stepping through the hole he had created.

The armoury was nothing special, but it held enough weapons for the four of them should the need arise. Gathering as much as he could, Clarke began handing rifles and magazines through to Rob without saying a word.

"What is going on?" Caroline asked, but her question was greeted by silence.

"Tell us," Nattie shouted, getting both Clarke's attention and a smile.

"We are going to go to war," he said before turning his attention to the handguns.

"I don't understand. You said the marines were coming to rescue us," Caroline said, her soft voice making her sound timid as the echo of Clarke's proclamation continued to reverberate down the hallways.

"The marines are coming, but I don't think it will be to save us. At least not me and Dennis. There must be something in here, in this bunker, that makes us a threat. We need to find out what it is before we make our stand." Clarke hopped back through the window and walked away from the group again. A man on a mission, he acted out of self-preservation.

Sliding behind one of the main consoles, Clarke began hammering at the keyboard, his large fingers punching the keyboard one letter at a time.

The group watched for a few minutes before the signs of Clarke's growing frustration became too painful to watch.

"Move over, let me have a go," Caroline said, shooing the big contractor away from the monitors.

Unlike Clarke, Caroline's fingers danced over the keyboard with a near silent grace, and before long, she had five different screens scrolling through different data sets.

"Fuck me," she said, drawing a surprised look from her colleagues and a laugh from Clarke.

"What have you found?" Clarke asked, leaning closer to the screens, as if the closer proximity would make sense of the scientific gibberish that was scrolling through them.

"I really don't think we should be reading this," she said, placing her hands on the desk.

"If they are coming to kill us, I would rather know what I'm dying to protect," Clarke said, his voice noticeably softer.

Caroline was quiet a moment, biting her bottom lip as her fingers strummed nervously against the lower edge of the keyboard. "Well, it looks like they were here long before we arrived. There are records here going back years. Best I can tell is they created the dinosaurs, and are trying to turn them into cyborgs or something. There are some older files that are corrupted. I see controls diagnostics over here. Genus and species information over there, and—" Caroline stopped.

"What is it?" Nattie asked, as the young woman turned to face her and Rob.

"They have all of our information here too. They were using us as a cover, to create hybrid dinosaurs." Caroline's face paled as she spoke.

"Why?" Rob asked, moving beside her, placing his arm around her shoulders as he read through the screens.

"It doesn't say, but I think it is pretty clear." Caroline looked up at him, tears welling in her eyes.

"Motherfuckers," Clark growled. "Building a frigging robot dinosaur army. Bloody Yanks. No offense," he added, looking at the three beside him.

"Woah, wait a minute. What's this?" Caroline said, pushing buttons as if she knew exactly what she was doing.

A few moments later, a large screen flickered to life on the main wall of the bunker. It flashed with static for a second before dividing into a grid of nine squares. Each one was a camera, showing different points of the island.

"Look, there," Rob pointed to the lower right screen. It showed two men standing by an entrance to the building. "Are they planting explosives?"

"Does that look like a rescue party?" Clarke picked up his rifle and began walking away.

"Hey, come back here, you can't even be thinking about going up there," Nattie called after Clarke.

"Stop him," Caroline called, her eyes glued to the screen. She jumped up from the chair and screamed. When she looked back at the screen, the camera was gone.

CHAPTER 30

The boat reached the shore, and under the cover of rapidly falling darkness, the two men scrambled up the rocky beach and onto the island.

Captain Kincaid brought the *Langley* round to the far, long side of the island, meaning the boat pulled up on the opposite side to where Clarke and his group had arrived. The compound was within a five-minute run from the shallow cliffs that rose from the beach.

Neither man spoke. Their mission was clear, and the room for interpretation was non-existent.

Gunnery Sergeant Plummer carried the charges that would give them entry to the building and down into the bunker. The plans rolled up in his gear confirmed the layout of the both the building and its bunker. He had them memorised and knew the quickest way in, down, and back out again. Sergeant Woods moved a little behind, his rifle raised. He swept from side to side, watching for any signs of movement.

The top secret papers they had been privy to proclaimed the island was deserted of dinosaur life. Aside from the bunker built by deep cover operatives working for Black Arrow Security, nobody had stepped foot onto the island, and an enforced segregation from the indigenous wildlife had been enforced thanks to the early control units implanted into the sea swelling creatures.

Still, it never hurt to take precautions.

"The building is ready. The charges have been placed," Plummer said, his voice a whisper, but rendered crystal clear in the earpiece that Woods wore.

"Roger that. It's all clear back here," Woods said from his position just inside the tree line.

"Make your way toward me, and we will blow this thing. Remember, the scientists need to come alive, the others, well, they are optional," Plummer said, making a point of reminding Woods about their objective.

He chose Woods for the mission because out of the four of them, he was the weak link. The youngest on the team, he had no blood on his hands, no real issues that told him the lay of the land. He needed to get dirty, and he needed to understand that sometimes, doing one's duty meant making sacrifices and hard calls.

"Copy that," Woods said as he broke into a run, crossing the cleared area around the building in a flash.

The ground rumbled, and the Tyrannosaurus appeared from the trees behind them. It emerged like a ghost from the trees. The presence of its arrival created a shadow that fell over the two men.

Plummer took his rifle and opened fire. Standing his ground, he unloaded a stream of hot lead into the creature, which roared at the inconvenience. Woods followed suit, backing up as he fired.

The creature lunged forward, its body seeming too large, and pitched too far forward to be stable, but somehow, it worked. The head swooped down and bit Woods in half. The rifle continued to fire from inside the creature's mouth.

What remained of Woods fell both left and the right with strands of intestine linking the remains together like laces on a shoe.

The dinosaur spun as the rifle fired bullets from inside its mouth. Its tail crashed against the wall, just as Plummer detonated the charge he had placed. The rear portion of the creature blew apart in a loud pop of blood and flesh.

With its tail gone, the Tyrannosaurs was pushed off balance and fell face first into the forest floor. Its head bouncing as it fell, it was unable to right itself as blood spurted in thick gushes that arced over and across the roof of the building.

Not wasting any time, Plummer slipped inside and made his way towards the bunker.

The power was out in the building, and the emergency lights were fading. The dimness was disorienting, but Plummer knew his way, even in pitch blackness. He had it memorized.

Clarke was waiting for him, his rifle raised and at the ready. He stood behind the door, knowing that the men coming for him would be preoccupied to think that they may have been spotted.

The first man appeared and moved straight to the trapdoor. He dropped the charges, and connected them all. A few moments later, they were two cracks that rang out. One that blew apart the locks on the bunker hatch, and the other that blew apart the large man's knee.

Emerging from the shadows, his face set in stone, Clarke raised the rifle and took careful aim at the injured man. His knee was gone, a bubbling mass of meat took its place. Yet he remained standing.

"You're a tough shit, aren't ya," Clarke spoke up, letting the full power of his native accent run wild.

Plummer turned his head, unable to mount anything of a comeback as it took all of his control to not pass out from the pain.

"What do you say, you drop them weapons and come with me," Clarke said, taking a step closer the Plummer. "That's right, all of it, Gunny, otherwise I'll take your other knee too."

Plummer dropped his weapons and found the ability to hop around so that he faced Clarke.

"Where's your mate? The other one that was with you?" Clarke turned his head to look through the door, but never once did the barrel of his rifle leave its focus point in the centre of Plummer's chest.

"He's dead. A rex ate him," Plummer growled through gritted teeth. Sweat poured from his head, which was turning an ever-deepening shade of red as he fought against the pain.

Clarke took one more look through the doorway before he slammed it closed. "Well, that makes this much easier then, mate." He walked up to Plummer, and without breaking his stride, slammed the butt of his rifle into the man's face. The squelch of his shattering nose sounded like a boot pulled from a gasping muddy puddle. It satisfied Clarke to the point where he left the man alone for the time being.

Carefully, he manoeuvred the body down the hatch and into the bunker, locking them back inside.

He dragged the bleeding body inside and let it lay where it fell upon his its release.

"We should put him in the infirmary," Nattie said, not even trying to hide her disdain.

"Nah, he won't live long enough to get benefit from treatment," Clarke answered, his eyes focusing on the screen. "Tell me what you have found."

Caroline said nothing for a moment, but looked to her peers. Nattie nodded, and Rob put a comforting hand on her shoulder.

"Well, it looks like this place was set up to do more than just protect people inside. You could control an entire country from here. I've got sensors and readings from well … pretty much anything you can think of. That guy there, he came from a ship, the *USS Langley*, they are sitting off shore waiting for them. There is also a submarine nearby, but they don't seem to be doing anything. These machines are basically feeding me this information; I don't even have to look for it," Caroline said, and her inner techie could not help but get excited, even against the backdrop of death and violence.

Clarke studied the young scientist, reading her excitement and enthusiasm. However, he was a man of the shadows. He knew what came next and did not know how to break it to them.

"I'm going to check on Dennis. Keep digging, see what you can find to help us out." He turned and walked back to the medical bay, stepping over the unconscious gunnery sergeant on the way.

Dennis looked bad. His body was pale, and the sweat dripping from him held the stench of sickness; the kind of lingering odour that clung to every surface inside a hospital. Not matter how clean, or how thoroughly scrubbed, the same stench remained, engrained into the building, right to the foundations.

He was shivering and looked to have lost half his body weight in the time he had been lying there.

"Looks like we have reached the end, buddy," Clarke said, moving next to the bed. "They've got the warships after us. Looks like we found the dirty secret of the modern day United States, and well, they don't want us telling anybody. I don't know if you can hear this, but, well, it's fucked up. You rest easy. You saved me back in the Sudan, and now it's my turn to save you." Clarke reached over to the table and took the bottle of morphine. He loaded the syringe to the max and injected it into Dennis's neck.

On the bed, Dennis stiffened and then convulsed for a moment before his body fell still. His breathing shallowed, slowed, and finally stopped. Clarke waited, saying a silent prayer for his dead friend.

He wiped his eyes with the back of his hand, only standing up when the inevitable sirens started to sound.

They blared like klaxons at a football stadium, the rising and falling pitch restless sea of noise. Clarke hurried back to the others.

"They just opened fire on us," Rob said, speaking as he turned.

CHAPTER 31

Philippe Mantle sat behind his desk as he did every day. His office was dark and windowless, the conditions cramped and claustrophobic, but he liked it that way. He had worked in the same place, in the same room, for almost fifteen years. He was great at his job, and had no ambitions for anything higher, nor plans to trade it in for a new setting or a change of pace. He liked order, and he liked routine. His small, dark corner of the world made him feel comfortable, and simply knowing it was there helped him when the size and scope of the real world threatened to become too much for him.

The fact that he did not know who he worked for, and that his pay cheque appeared in his bank every two weeks with a variety of different names attached to it, did little to bother him. He knew the work he did, and could make assumptions as to what level of security he held, but he held no inclination to do so.

So when an alarm starting ringing on his machine, announcing the presence of people inside of Crichton Labs override security system, Phillipe knew he was in for a bad day; a day that would mess with the schedule he liked to stick to. It angered him. Picking up his phone, he already felt on edge about the disruption.

"Sir, this is Phillippe, somebody has activated the Crichton security system. They are poking around, aimlessly if I look at it, but they are getting close to finding Trix," Phillipe spoke to his supervisor, the faceless man who only ever communicated via the telephone.

Phillippe listened to the voice on the other end of the phone and hung up. "Yes, sir," he managed to add before the line went dead.

Phillippe moved back to his computer and got to work trying to find out more about their uninvited guests.

***

Sikke Werkhoven moved through Johan's house, stopping off in the library where he casually plucked a first edition book from the shelves, and a bottle of aged whiskey from the cabinet, and made his way out the front door.

The helicopter flew up and over the house. Sikke looked up, shielding his eyes, watching the bird move over the coast before turning back to the sea.

He gave a sigh and turned back to the house. It was a stunning property. Maybe he would buy it once the damage had been corrected.

The shrill tone of his phone made him jump. It broke the recently re-settled silence like a siren.

"I am disappointed, Director," the disguised voice spoke, cutting Sikke off before he could even truly answer the device. "I thought you could handle the job at Crichton Labs, but evidently I was mistaken. It shall not happen again."

"Sir," Sikke began, but the line went dead.

Sikke never saw the red sight on the back of his head, nor the assassin that lay in wait. He did hear the quiet whoosh of the silenced weapon, and felt the cool ocean breeze tickle his exposed brain, but then everything went black.

CHAPTER 32

Lieutenant Lloyd stood on the bridge of the *Langley* and watched as his CO walked back onto the bridge. He cut a dejected figure. It was the image of a man who had received either a telling off for something he was not responsible for in the first place, or even worse, a man who had been tasked with cleaning up the mess said people had left behind.

"How's it looking, Captain?" Lloyd asked, waiting until his CO was close enough to keep the conversation between the two of them.

"It's looking like the back end of the lord mayor's parade," Kincaid said.

"I don't understand," Lloyd said, knowing that the captain would occasionally throw in expressions learned during his years of education in England.

"It means it's a pile of shit. Get the *Anderson* on comms, and ready the missiles," Kincaid spoke with authority, and a tone that told his XO not to both asking any more questions.

"Aye, sir." Lloyd turned and walked away. "Sir, Captain Defour is on comms."

"Captain, I just received a call from the pentagon. You are to regroup with us at the rear of the island. We have orders to open fire on the compound." The words echoed around the bridge with the finality of a hangman's snapping noose.

"Captain," Lloyd began, but one look from his CO silenced him.

"We have our orders, and we will see them through," Kincaid spoke. "Captain Defour, I need you to start moving now."

"Sir, what about Plummer and Woods?" Lloyd asked, his voice calling across the bridge.

"They are to be presumed dead. Our orders are from the highest level, Lieutenant, and we are expected to follow them through.

"Yes, sir," Lloyd answered, lowering his gaze. He could hear the stress in his CO's voice and realized it would be unwise to push the matter any further.

"Lieutenant, you have the bridge," Kincaid said. Turning to leave, he leaned over to one of the technicians near him, and a few moments later took two cigarettes from the pack offered to him.

The air on deck was cool and crisp. The breeze whisked away the smoke from his cigarette. Standing on the deck, he watched the crew as they ran through the motions. He felt a surging pride in knowing they were following his orders, that he had trained his ship to run in such a well-oiled fashion. It also stung, knowing that those men were jumping to his word, when he himself had no idea what they were doing. Launching missiles to take out a military institution. In Kincaid's mind, that was an act of terrorism, the very thing he enlisted to fight.

His head spun, and not only from his first cigarette in over six years.

"Captain, the missiles are primed and ready," John Pike, the chief weapons officer, said. Approaching the captain, he leaned against the railing and looked out at the island. "I reckon I know what you are thinking."

Captain Kincaid gave a snorted laugh and turned to face the officer. Pike was the oldest and most experienced man on the ship, and regardless of regulations, that earned him certain privileges in Kincaid's eyes.

"Enlighten me, Mr. Pike," Kincaid said, tossing the butt of his cigarette overboard.

"You're thinking that this makes us terrorists, probably even wondering if this is a set-up. You're going to start questioning what we are doing, and what you believe in," Pike spoke in quiet, relaxed tones, his eyes never leaving the islands.

"You might just be psychic," Kincaid laughed.

"Nah, just an old son of a bitch who has seen and heard plenty of things over the years. With all due respect, Captain, those fears are valid, but they are not the issue. They are just your own hang ups, and trust me, they are good problems to have. What you really need to be worried about is what have we created on that island that is so bad, the folks back home are willing to destroy it now?" Pike turned and looked at his captain, who returned his look in silence. "Like I said, the missiles are ready for your orders, sir."

Pike walked away, and Kincaid was alone again. For a moment, he even wondered if he had imagined everything. The walk back to the bridge had him feeling conflicted, but by the time he reached the captain's chair, his mind was resolved. He knew what needed to be done.

"Mr. Pike," he spoke into the comms.

"Aye, sir."

"Fire when ready." Kincaid stood to attention as the boat shook as the RIM-161 missile took to the sky. They traced its path until impact, when a cloud of dust obscured the island before the fireball of the explosion flared on their screens.

CHAPTER 33

The alarms rang and sent Caroline into a panic. She jumped up from the computer terminal and into Rob's arms.

"I didn't touch anything," she said, spitting words in rapid fire as her fear skyrocketed.

"Shit. Everybody hold onto something," Clarke called just moments before the entire bunker shook. The ear-splitting roar from above shook them to their boots. The computer terminals rattled and several sparked and burst from the force of the impact above them.

The echo of the blast reverberated through the bunker, while seeming to retain its depth and fear-inspiring resonance.

The temperature in the small underground room rose substantially, while the air felt as if it were drying up around them.

Eventually, the rumble stopped, and while the dust swirled in the air of the bunker, it seemed they had survived. For now.

"What was that?" Nattie asked, picking herself up from the half-crouched positon she had curled into.

"That was a missile strike. I guess the orders have changed. They must really not want us finding whatever it is they are hiding down here," Clark said, his voice filled with steely conviction. "Caroline, I need you behind this machine. There is something we missed. Something they don't want us to see. A file, and experiment, maybe even a weapon."

Caroline raised her head, but did not let go of Rob. "I did see something," she said slowly, her words careful, and thoughtful.

"Then find it. We won't have long before they hit us again, and while this place was built like a fortress, it has its limits."

"Okay, hold on." Caroline sat back behind the computers, her hands no longer dancing over the keys, but stabbing at them with a slow and methodical caution, as if any one of them could be a trap, a switch they would kill them all, or release a volley of nuclear weapons across the globe.

On the floor, Plummer groaned, but nobody paid him any mind. If he was there with them, then his fate was sealed also.

"I saw something, I know I did, but I can't find it … I can't. Oh God. I don't want to die." Caroline began to weep behind the console.

Rob moved to comfort her, but it was Clarke that crouched down first.

"Listen to me," he said, his words firm but soft. "You can do this. You can find this thing and maybe, just maybe, we can use it to bargain our way out of here. Just stay calm, focus, and remember, death is not to be feared. The only thing we should be worried about it missing out on chances while we were alive. Now think about where we are. For right or wrong, we got to work with real live dinosaurs. That is something pretty special if you ask me."

Caroline sniffed and wiped her tears away with the back of her hands.

"You're right." She fell silent a while, her eyes catching something. "Here it is. Look, it's a sub folder call Trix. It struck me as weird because it doesn't match anything else."

"Let's take a look and see what we have," Clarke said, a smile threatening to stretch across his lips, and hope sounding in his words.

CHAPTER 34

The smoke cleared and the flare of the blast died down. The island looked in shambles. The trees and vegetation were gone, reduced to nothing more than smouldering piles of charcoal.

"It was a direct hit sir, the building has been destroyed," XO Lloyd spoke up, turning toward his captain.

"Very good, Lieutenant. Prepare to fire a second wave," Kincaid spoke without breaking a beat. He had opened fire, and made the first steps that would either make his career, or end it. He did not see the point in leaving it at a single pace when he could run toward his destiny, fearless.

"Sir, the island has been—" Lloyd began.

"The bunker is designed to withstand a single missile attack. I want us to hit it with everything we have. Load up the RIMs and open fire when ready. No need for my command." Kincaid raised his voice on the bridge, for what was only the third time in his memory.

"Yes, sir," Lloyd said, his face reddening.

"Thank you, Lieutenant. Tell me, where is the *Anderson?*"

"The *Anderson* is coming into position now. They are two clicks to the east. They will be ready to fire at your signal, sir."

"Wonderful. If that bunker survives the RIM strikes, then their cruise missiles will be out last chance without having to send in a whole damn team on foot." The pressure was starting to get to the captain, whose cool and calm demeanour slipped further with every battling step they took.

"Missiles are ready, Captain," a faceless voice echoed around the bridge.

Kincaid said nothing. He merely stood, with his eyes fixed on the island.

A few moments later, the boat shook as the final three RIM-161 missiles flew from the launcher.

They streaked through the sky and pummelled the ground, each one landing within as small a distance of each other as was possible.

The island disappeared behind a spreading dark grey, near black cloud of destruction. Captain Kincaid did not flinch at the sight, but felt the weight of each detonation weighing down on his shoulders.

CHAPTER 35

Noise exploded through the bunker, which rattled and shook. The walls racked and the acrid smell of smoke and explosives began to fill the airtight space. The first blast had knocked out the air supply, which meant they were living on borrowed time. The pollutants that were now added to the mix only meant the countdown moved at a faster pace.

"Keep going," Clarke said, as the computer screen flicked on and off. "The power for this place is beneath us. We will be dead before these computers are."

"I have it, I just don't understand a damned thing about what it is saying. I mean, it looks like … no, it can't be possible." Caroline's language skills quickly dropped to nonsensical ramblings, which prompted both Rob and Nattie to lean in closer to the screen.

"Good God," Nattie said, taking a step back. "That's not possible."

"Would someone fucking explain things to me?" Clarke shouted, hoping to bring their focus back to the task at hand.

"Trix is a special program they were working on. It turns out that certain experiments were at a more advanced stage than others. Their impulse and neurological control experiments were already at an advanced stage of real-life testing. The science behind it is clunky, unreliable to say the least, but heck, it's nearly fifteen years old," Nattie said, explaining the situation, but much to Clarke's annoyance, she did not give any actual answers.

He opened his mouth to speak when a second console next to them came to life. It was a single screen with what looked to be a joystick control system. Two buttons connected to the stick, which made Clarke think about the controls of the early jets he had trained in.

The screen flickered to life, shaking as whatever the camera was mounted on rocked back and forth.

"Holy shit, look," Rob said, pointing to the screen.

"I think I woke her up," Caroline said, sounding apologetic.

"What, who … will one of you give me some damned answers?" Clarke roared, his patience worn thin and through.

"You wanted a miracle to save us, Mr. Clarke, and I think we just found it," Nattie answered, as Rob slid behind the joystick-controlled station.

"Watch and learn," Rob spoke, his words suddenly cocky and brash. "It looks just like a computer game," he said as he took the control. "Responsiveness is crap."

"Wait, let me try something," Caroline answered. It was as if Clarke no longer existed. His gruff words and impatient growls fell on deaf ears.

Nattie looked at him and smiled. "At least we will go out with a bang."

The image on the screen changed. The camera rose in unsteady, jerky movements.

"Wait, that's … that's the building on the main island," Clarke said, his eyes glued to the screen. "This camera, it must be in the volcano, but why?"

He muttered under his breath, trying to put the pieces together, no knowing that the others were not only farther ahead than him, but on a totally different puzzle.

"No, the camera is on Trix. She was in the volcano, but right now, she is heading our way," Rob said, his face and words tense through concentration. "Just watch the other screens and tell me when you see her."

Clarke was lost, but understood enough to know the lab geeks were now in charge. He was obsolete.

"What the hell is that?" Clarke spat pointing at the central camera on the large main screen.

The shape moved fast, flying on large wings that looked to be more metal than flesh. They beat with a strange, robotic awkwardness.

"Say hello to Trix," Rob said, speaking through pursed lips.

"No, are you shitting me?" Clarke spat, falling into the chair behind him.

"Nope. Say hello to the world first remote-controlled cyborg dinosaur," Rob laughed as he spoke. "I wonder what Trix stands for. It's always an acronym with these projects."

Even though their discovery had not changed the nature of their predicament, the mood had been lifted. There could be no denying it.

"Is that thing, alive?" Clarke asked.

"I don't know. There are readings here, but they don't make much sense. I think the sensors are either broken or not powered up yet," Caroline said, her hands once again dancing a merry tune over the keys. "But she does have a few surprises up her sleeve."

"Such as?" Clarke asked, his interest coming out a little too enthusiastic for such a big man.

"For instance, she has shoulder cannons mounted onto her wings," Caroline said, reading the information as it appeared on her screen.

"Fuck," Clarke whistled, clapping his hands together.

Nattie fell into the chair beside him. "Doesn't this just all seem a little odd? Remote-controlled dinosaurs, cyborg battle plans."

"Hey, I didn't write this thing. It's just the way it is. Who are we to argue with that?" Clarke said, not wanting to spend too much time thinking about the how or the why of their situation.

"I guess, but it doesn't make any sense. None of this does," Nattie argued. As a scientist, she preferred to work with logic and fact. They were comforting in their certainty.

"It doesn't, but that is life, I guess. It doesn't make sense; it isn't some planned-out work of fiction. Things happen, shit happens, and more often than not, there is no explanation for it," Clarke answered, getting as philosophical as he ever had, or would. "Now, turn that thing out to sea. Let's give those boats a scare and see if we can't make them turn tail and run."

"Well, she has the turning circle of an oil tanker, but she is coming around," Rob said, straining as he fought the controls. "They will need to improve on this if they ever want it to work."

"I see the boat on the screen. What do you want me to do?" Rob asked, confused.

"Blow it out of the fucking water," Clarke roared.

CHAPTER 36

"Sir, we have an incoming bogey showing up on the radar," the technician called out, caught by surprise at the sudden emergence of the signal.

"I need some details," Captain Kincaid said as he hurried over to the radar station.

"Well, it could be an anomaly. I mean, it just appeared on the screen. It doesn't seem to have come from anywhere, but ... well, it's enormous, and closing in on our location," the young man spoke.

"Bring me the video feeds," Captain Kincaid called. "And get gunners on the cannons. I want to be ready for anything."

The bridge burst into life as a flurry of war-readying activities were acted out. The silence returned the minute the video screen appeared, and everybody saw what they were fighting against.

As the bridge crew stood in stunned silence, two flashes flared on either side of the monstrous creature baring down on them.

Alarms began to ring on the bridge as the two small calibre missiles closed the distance on the boat.

"I want those guns online now," Kincaid roared as the *Langley* was rocked by two explosions. One hit the front of the craft, tearing a hole in the deck, twisting the metal as it punctured the boat's surface. The damage was superficial, but if enough was inflicted, the boat would be crippled.

The second missile blasted into the upper decks, taking out the officer's mess and shaking the bridge.

Sparks flew as computers short circuited. People screamed, and jumped back as electric currents shot from consoles into their bodies.

"Status report," Captain Kincaid called.

"Guns are online and ready to fire on your command, Captain," one voice replied.

"Damage is minimal. Superficial for the most part, but we lost the short-range sonar," another replied.

One by one, the picture was painted of their situation, and the realization hit that the *Langley* was at war.

"Raise the *Anderson*, tell them to fire when ready. We will deal with this hell beast," Kincaid called, just as the deck-mounted cannons began to rattle off round after round of high-speed lead, dealing death in strafing waves as the gunners chose quantity over accuracy.

***

"Fuck yeah, look at that," Rob cried out as the missiles impacted on the destroyer.

The aiming mechanism was shaky at best, and he had not expected either, let alone both, of the missiles to find their target.

"Watch out," Clarke called, caught up in the rush of battle.

The two main mounted guns turned and sent volley after volley of fire at Trix, who dropped out of the sky, missing the strafed shots.

"Nice move," Caroline said as she continued to read about Trix, and the list of things she could do.

"It was an accident. I lost power for a moment," Rob replied.

"This is fascinating. Their plans are utterly insane, but the possibilities, the implications ..." Caroline said, lost to the draw of research.

"Hey, don't forget, they are the bad guys right now," Clarke said. "Move around to the rear, come at it from behind. You want to take out the towers. Get rid of their comms."

"Sure thing," Rob answered, pushing the joystick hard to the right. "This thing is clunky as fuck," he grumbled to himself.

***

"Sir, she has moved behind us."

"Bring us around, full speed, let's draw this son of a bitch out to sea," Captain Kincaid roared. "Bring the CIWS online and get the SRBOC loaded and ready. Let's make this difficult for them."

Time seemed to slow down, the stress of the situation bringing out the best in the *Langley's* crew.

"CIWS is online, sir."

"Sir, the aviators have two SeaHawks fully loaded and ready to go, on your orders," Lieutenant Lloyd said, relaying the message from the hangars.

"Get them airborne. If they want to make a fight of this, then we will give them a fight." Kincaid slammed his fist into his open palm. "Any news from the *Anderson*?"

"Sir, the *Anderson* is almost in position, and ready to fire," the communications officer called, his voice strengthened by surging adrenaline.

***

"Sir, we are clear to fire on the target," the communications officer on the *Anderson* called through the Captain Defour.

Standing in front of the periscope screen, Captain Defour watched as the two helicopters took off from the deck of the *Langley*. Everything seemed too surreal to be true. An island filled with dinosaurs. Cyborg-like creatures of their own design being used against them. None of it made any sense.

"Very well. Fire when ready," Defour called out as the submarine rose to the surface once more.

"Sir, that creature is getting pretty close again," his XO said as he stood in discussion with a terrified-looking sonar operator.

"Leave it to the *Langley*, we have our orders," Defour answered.

"No, sir, I mean the creature underwater," the young technician answered.

Defour froze for a moment. "Ready the forward torpedoes. Fire on my mark. I will not strike if it is not necessary."

"Sir, missiles are preparing to launch." A shudder ran through the sub as the Tomahawk missile rose into the air. The vertical launch took the missile out of view before it began its looping descent toward its target.

***

Sergeant How pulled his SeaHawk into a sharp left turn, sweeping low to the destroyer, moving between the bursts of gun fire.

Having watched the creatures on the island, he thought he had seen it all. The devices attached to them had looked like something from a science fiction movie, and a bad one at that. Now he found himself taking his bird into a dogfight with a prehistoric robosaurus.

Behind him, Sergeant Langston moved into position behind their GAU-15 .50 calibre machine gun.

Behind them, the ship's second SeaHawk took off in the opposite direction, turning directly into the path of the creature. Their gunner opened fire, spraying round after round into the air.

The robosaurus rose steeply, rising above the helo, before stabilizing its position, and firing two missiles from its shoulder-mounted cannons.

The projectiles sped towards the attacking helicopter, which rose and turned to avoid the first missile, while firing a burst of rounds into the exposed flank of living tissue. While the wings and upper body appeared to be predominantly mechanical, the creature was definitely soft in the flank.

The creature flinched and unleased a booming shriek. The second missile curled around the helo and slammed into it just beneath the rotor. The explosion tore the rotorcraft apart and sent the fuselage tumbling into the ocean below.

One chunk crashed into the ocean while the other crashed onto the *Langley*, tearing through the helipad, creating a crater in the deck like an impacting meteorite.

Shards of the destroyed rotor blades were sent spinning in all directions, with one wedging itself into the creature's gut, eliciting another pained roar from the beast.

Having heard the explosion, Sergeant How swung his helo around in a tight circle.

"Be ready," he called back to his gunner.

The instant the beast came into range, Langston opened fire.

***

"I can't control it," Rob cried out. His face was red from fighting the controls, his hands slicked with sweat.

"What do you mean?" Nattie asked.

"I mean it's not responding. They shot it, and now it's not responding," Rob replied, his voice strained from exertion.

"Well, we gave it our best shot," Clarke answered, his eyes not on the dogfight, but on the submarine. He rose moments before firing on the island. By Clarke's estimate, they were onto borrowed time.

"What do you mean?" Caroline asked. She started to turn, but never finished the motion.

The impact shook the bunker and cracked open the ceiling. With the main building levelled, they were exposed and vulnerable.

The explosion started as a whoosh of air being sucked out of the room. For a few moments, which felt like minutes, they could not breathe, and then it returned as a wind, rushing against them with a force that knocked Clarke to the floor.

The room fell apart around them, and the flames engulfed their bodies. While the bunker still shielded them from a large portion of the blast, it was not enough to save them. Clarke disappeared, his body torn apart by the force of the rushing wind. Nattie followed, the skin flying from her body as if being flailed by some invisible assailant. Blood sprayed in all directions in a firework of gore. She screamed and dropped to the floor, her body finally exploding, bursting like a swollen zit.

The flames followed, riding on the back of a rolling thunder clap, multiplied by a thousand.

Rob tried to move, to take Caroline into his arms, but instead, he watched her burn. Her body caught like a candle wick, and in the brief moment between her incineration, and his, he was forced to watch her body melt. Skin bubbled and peeled away while her eyes burst in an instant, like eggs hitting a hot pan.

His body caught a moment later, the flames blinding him before he followed Caroline's fate.

Nothing was saved from the blast. The computers and equipment were destroyed, and the two other bodies that filled the bunker, those of Dennis Blankenstijn and the unconscious Gunner Sergeant Plummer, were reduced to nothing but ash, the same as their counterparts.

The walls of the bunker crumbled, the steel supports buckling and twisting as the heat of the blast melted them and their concrete coating.

CHAPTER 37

Sergeant How saw the explosion bloom before them as he followed the robosaurus. Langston had torn a hole in its flank as they passed within close range of one another. Since then, the change in the creature's behaviour was great. It flew with purpose, as if the living side had taken control.

"We need to steer clear of the blast," How called back to Langston. "Hold on."

They made a tight turn and rose into a steep climb. Alarms began to ring in the cockpit and when they levelled off, How saw why. A dark cloud moved towards them from the central island.

"Holy shit," he cried as the group of pteranodon's flew closer. He counted six in all, four of which moved on the direction of the robosaurus.

"Take those things down," How called just as Langston opened fire, the .50 calibre guns spewing death in all directions.

One of the creatures that headed towards the chopper exploded in a shower of blood and gore. Dipping down low, they turned and avoided the falling chunks of meat, which pelted the ocean like cannonballs.

Above the islands, the four pteranodons met the robosaurus head on. How was at a loss to explain why they attacked it, but attack they did, sweeping in on it in a group formation.

"Why is it not firing its weapons?" Langston asked, caught up in the fight and seemingly disappointed at the lack of action.

"Like I fucking know," How growled back to him.

"Let's swing around and come back at them from the other side," How suggested, not waiting for the offer to be discussed.

Below them, the *Langley* limped away, its rear low in the water, the damage from the impact with the SeaHawk severe, but unlikely to stop them from regrouping with the carrier group.

The *Anderson* had disappeared, although they could make out the streaks of white foam left in the wake of the two torpedoes they had just fired.

***

"Captain, the creature is turning. Its speed is increasing, twenty-five knots, up from twenty," the sonar technician called out.

Captain Defour turned. "Take us down," he ordered and the submarine began to descend.

"Sir, still closing, speed twenty-seven knots. Time to impact is four minutes."

"We need to act now," XO Burke spoke in a quiet, but serious tone.

"Fire torpedoes, and increase out speed," Defour called, cutting his XO off.

The submarine growled as the two MK-48 torpedoes sped away from the craft. The shallow depth made the sub rock harder that anybody anticipated and had the crew on the bridge reaching out to hold their balance.

The fish sped towards their target. The first struck head on with the charging aquatic dinosaur, blowing a hole through its head, spilling blood, bone, and brain into the water. The second buried itself in the flank of the twisted beast, ripping it apart from front flipper to rear limb, spilling guts and an endless stream of thick black-coloured intestines into the water.

"Direct hit, sir. The target is down," the sonar technician advised. There was no cheering on the bridge this time.

"Very good. Let's turn this thing around and head back to the *Langley*. They are going to need some assistance," Captain Defour replied.

***

By the time How had circled around the smoking mass of burned-out ground that had been the third island, the robosaurus had taken care of three of the pteranodons that had attacked it and was busy dispatching of the fourth. The creature was clearly of their species, but its gargantuan size and the metalwork that covered so much of its body, including the robotic enhancements to its wings, made it a target; like the odd one out in the playground.

Its large beak opened, revealing rows of serrated teeth, each one several inches long. A single snap and it wrenched a wing from the pteranodon, which spiralled down into the ocean, spraying blood in all directions. The creature crashed into the sea, just as the torpedoes found their mark. Its screaming carcass splashed down in time with the eruption, making quite the spectacle.

In the time it took for the pteranodon to drop, the robosaurus charged. Its body was injured, blood dribbled from its wounds, while the severed section of helicopter blade still protruded from its gut.

The creature closed the gap on the chopper, its body impacting with the nose while its large metallic wings closed around either side. Everything went dark as its body blocked the windows.

Langston opened fire, sending a burst of .50 calibre lead into creature that attacked them like the giant squid attacking the *Nautilus*.

Sparks lit up the cabin as hot lead met reinforced metal. Holes appeared in the wing, and blood dripped through from where metal and flesh combined. Yet the robosaurus did not let go. Its beak broke through the cockpit windshield and pierced Sergeant How's chest. His body tensed as the beak opened, slowly spreading the puncture wound.

How tried to scream but all that came out was blood, a thick torrent of copper-tainted liquid. How heard his ribs snap, one by one, as his chest was opened up like a heart patient on the operating table.

"Hey, motherfucker!" Langston screamed. He stood in the cockpit, a shotgun in his hands. He held the weapon low and gave a smile.

"I'm all out of bubble gum, bitch," Langston laughed. He had always wanted to be able to use a one liner. He fired the shotgun and the creature's face caved inwards. Blood and meat bubbled to the surface. Adjusting his aim, Langston fired once again, and the creature's head exploded. Its beak jerked open in a spasm of death, and How's chest burst. Fragments of rib flew through the air like throwing stars, peppering Langston with bone shrapnel.

The creature fell away, pulling the chopper with it. The sudden change in pitch threw him forward and into the bloody mess that had been the robosaurus's head.

The chopper spun several times as it fell, dropping out of the sky, pulled straight down by the weight of the robotic beast clamped onto its nose.

The aircraft crashed into the sea, at points between the *Anderson* and the *Langley*, the robosaurus disappearing along with it, sinking to the seabed.

When the dust settled, and the seas calmed, the two navy vessels sat still, both the worse for wear following their engagements, the wounds of battle fresh for all to see. Nobody understood what had happened, what they had seen, or what they had done. Nobody knew why, but all understood it was not their place to question it. They had received their orders, and they saw to it that they were completed.

THE END

CHECK OUT OTHER GREAT DINOSAUR THRILLERS

WRITTEN IN STONE
by David Rhodes

Charles Dawson is trapped 100 million years in the past. Trying to survive from day to day in a world of dinosaurs he devises a plan to change his fate. As he begins to write messages in the soft mud of a nearby stream, he can only hope they will be found by someone who can stop his time travel. Professor Ron Fontana and Professor Ray Taggit, scientists with opposing views, each discover the fossilized messages. While attempting to save Charles, Professor Fontana, his daughter Lauren and their friend Danny are forced to join Taggit and his group of mercenaries. Taggit does not intend to rescue Charles Dawson, but to force Dawson to travel back in time to gather samples for Taggit's fame and fortune. As the two groups jump through time they find they must work together to make it back alive as this fast-paced thriller climaxes at the very moment the age of dinosaurs is ending.

HARD TIME
by Alex Laybourne

Rookie officer Peter Malone and his heavily armed team are sent on a deadly mission to extract a dangerous criminal from a classified prison world. A Kruger Correctional facility where only the hardest, most vicious criminals are sent to fend for themselves, never to return.

But when the team come face to face with ancient beasts from a lost world, their mission is changed. The new objective: Survive.

SEVEREDPRESS

CHECK OUT OTHER GREAT DINOSAUR THRILLERS

SPINOSAURUS
by Hugo Navikov

Brett Russell is a hunter of the rarest game. His targets are cryptids, animals denied by science. But they are well known by those living on the edges of civilization, where monsters attack and devour their animals and children and lay ruin to their shantytowns.

When a shadowy organization sends Brett to the Congo in search of the legendary dinosaur cryptid Kasai Rex, he will face much more than a terrifying monster from the past. Spinosaurus is a dinosaur thriller packed with intrigue, action and giant prehistoric predators.

LAND OF DEATH
by Eric S Brown & Alex Laybourne

A group of American soldiers, fleeing an organized attack on their base camp in the Middle East, encounter a storm unlike anything they've seen before. When the storm subsides, they wake up to find themselves no longer in the desert and perhaps not even on Earth. The jungle they've been deposited in is a place ruled by prehistoric creatures long extinct. Each day is a struggle to survive as their ammo begins to run low and virtually everything they encounter, in this land they've been hurled into, is a deadly threat.

CHECK OUT OTHER GREAT DINOSAUR THRILLERS

JURASSIC ISLAND
by Viktor Zarkov

Guided by satellite photos and modern technology a ragtag group of survivalists and scientists travel to an uncharted island in the remote South Indian Ocean. Things go to hell in a hurry once the team reaches the island and the massive megalodon that attacked their boats is only the beginning of their desperate fight for survival.

Nothing could have prepared billionaire explorer Joseph Thornton and washed up archaeologist Christopher "Colt" McKinnon for the terrifying prehistoric creatures that wait for them on JURASSIC ISLAND!

K-REX
by L.Z. Hunter

Deep within the Congo jungle, Circuitz Mining employs mercenaries as security for its Coltan mining site. Armed with assault rifles and decades of experience, nothing should go wrong. However, the dangers within the jungle stretch beyond venomous snakes and poisonous spiders. There is more to fear than guerrillas and vicious animals. Undetected, something lurks under the expansive treetop canopy . . .

Something ancient.

Something dangerous.

Kasai Rex!

CHECK OUT OTHER GREAT DINOSAUR THRILLERS

THE VALLEY
by Rick Jones

In a dystopian future, a self-contained valley in Argentina serves as the 'far arena' for those convicted of a crime. Inside the Valley: carnivorous dinosaurs generated from preserved DNA. The goal: cross the Valley to get to the Gates of Freedom. The chance of survival: no one has ever completed the journey. Convicted of crimes with little or no merit, Ben Peyton and others must battle their way across fields filled with the world's deadliest apex predators in order to reach salvation. All the while the journey is caught on cameras and broadcast to the world as a reality show, the deaths and killings real, the macabre appetite of the audience needing to be satiated as Ben Peyton leads his team to escape not only from a legal system that's more interested in entertainment than in justice, but also from the predators of the Valley.

JURASSIC DEAD
by Rick Chesler & David Sakmyster

An Antarctic research team hoping to study microbial organisms in an underground lake discovers something far more amazing: perfectly preserved dinosaur corpses. After one thaws and wakes ravenously hungry, it becomes apparent that death, like life, will find a way.
Environmental activist Alex Ramirez, son of the expedition's paleontologist, came to Antarctica to defend the organisms from extinction, but soon learns that it is the human race that needs protecting.

www.ingramcontent.com/pod-product-compliance
Lightning Source LLC
Chambersburg PA
CBHW032001170626
46807CB00006B/2597